A Light

A Bushel of Light

TROON HARRISON

Stoddart Kids
TORONTO · NEW YORK

YA
Har

Published in Canada in 2000 by
Stoddart Kids,
a division of Stoddart Publishing Co. Limited
34 Lesmill Road
Toronto, Canada M3B 2T6
Tel (416) 445-3333 Fax (416) 445-5967
E-mail cservice@genpub.com

Published in the United States in 2001 by
Stoddart Kids,
a division of Stoddart Publishing Co. Limited
180 Varick Street, 9th Floor
New York, New York 10014
Toll free 1-800-805-1083
E-mail gdsinc@genpub.com

Distributed in Canada by
General Distribution Services
325 Humber College Blvd.
Toronto, Canada M9W 7C3
Tel (416) 213-1919 Fax (416) 213-1917
E-mail cservice@genpub.com

Distributed in the United States by
General Distribution Services, PMB 128
4500 Witmer Industrial Estates
Niagara Falls, New York 14305-1386
Toll free 1-800-805-1083
E-mail gdsinc@genpub.com

04 03 02 01 00 1 2 3 4 5

Canadian Cataloguing in Publication Data

Harrison, Troon, 1958-
A bushel of light

ISBN 0-7737-6140-3

I. Title.

PS8565.A6587B87 2000   jC813'.54   C99-932565-5
PZ7.H37Bu 2000

Cover painting: Julia Bell
Cover and text design: Tannice Goddard

*We acknowledge for their financial support of our publishing program the
Government of Canada through the Book Publishing Industry Development
Program (BPIDP), the Canada Council, and the Ontario Arts Council.*

Printed and bound in Canada

For Chris —

*who shares my journeys and has
faith I'll reach my destinations.*

ACKNOWLEDGMENTS

The author wishes to thank the Ontario Arts Council for financial support.

Thanks to Stephen Brown and Eugenie Fernandes who have nurtured my growth as a writer; to Ivy Sucee, Chairperson of the Hazelbrae Barnardo Memorial Group, for checking my historical accuracy; to the Peterborough women writers for their friendship (Jane Bow, Mary Breen, Lea Harper, Julie Johnston, Patricia Stone, Betsy Struthers, Florence Treadwell, Christl Verduyn); and most of all to my sister Gwedhen and my parents for their constant, loving encouragement.

A Bushel of Light

CHAPTER
ONE

She was looking in through my window again — that girl with the hair like mine, hair that was turning from golden to plain dark red as the rain soaked into it. Drops ran down her face, too. Or maybe they were tears. Whatever they were, they darkened her freckles, which were usually the color of pale sand. Like mine.

I wished she would go away. Wind whipped her thin shawl around her shoulders. Her blue eyes were wide open, looking in at me accusingly. Behind her, the waves were running across the bay with white horses on them, the way they did when there was a northeast wind. They would be leaping against the lighthouse. The fishing boats would be running for harbor, water crashing up under their bows.

The girl spread her palms flat on my window. Her fingers were long and pale. Her mouth opened and her lips moved, shaping words.

"I can't hear you!" I shouted at her. "Go away!" I was sure now that it was tears making her face so wet. She pressed the tip of her nose against the glass. The pale, green glass that was always between us, streaming with cold rain.

I was going to start crying myself if she didn't leave.

"Get up, you lazy baggage!" Willy's voice broke into my consciousness. I hauled myself to a sitting position even before my eyes were open, and then grabbed the toe of Willy's boot.

"Get this out of my ribs," I said. I tightened my hold on his boot and shoved backwards. Willy kicked as he tore his foot from my grasp, and I knew there would be a bruise on my wrist later. My bewildering dream was still swirling around in my head, pictures of waves and rain. Completely ridiculous as I was sitting in a hot, Canadian field at haying time. I shook my head.

"You're no better'n a hired hand around here," Willy said. "You better be remembering not to sleep when you should be working. Lunch is over, Maggie."

I glared up at him. He was a little older and a little taller than me, but not much. He had bony arms, and his narrow eyes were set in a long face. Whenever he was being mean, which was almost always, his eyes got even narrower. And when he told lies, they looked off sideways somewhere.

"That dress is getting too small for you," he said with a snicker. "Or maybe you're just gettin' too big for the dress. Could be that's the real problem."

I glanced down. My face burned as I fumbled with a button that had come undone on my chest. When I looked at Willy, he snickered again. There was something about the way he looked at me these days that made a cold fist in my stomach.

I stood up silently, with strands of hay clinging to my dress and my tin lunch pail empty beside me. I hadn't meant to fall asleep, but the heat had made me drowsy. I looked around for Lizzy. She was close by, sitting on the stone fence and singing to herself. Her short, pudgy legs kicked to and fro as she twisted a piece of hay around a bunch of wilted clover. Further away, the team of horses stood patiently in the middle of the field. Sunlight flashed off their harness buckles. Their nose bags hung limp and empty.

"Get a move on then," said Willy.

I ignored him, even when he stuck out a foot to trip me as I walked away. My hay fork was leaning against the wagon. Its handle was smooth and warm. Funny how something so smooth could make blisters all over my hands by the end of a week in the hay. I stabbed the fork into the long swathes of cut, dry grass. It smelled as sweet as wildflowers and blue sky. In one quick motion, I lifted the fork and tossed the hay onto the wagon.

Tom came across the field towards me. He was the hired man and he walked like a hound dog. His joints were all loose and his legs shambled over the ground as if they weren't sure which direction to take. They never looked like they were moving very fast, but they were long and he was beside me in no time.

"Workin' by yourself," he commented, shaking his curly hair disapprovingly.

I glanced towards the fence. Willy was talking to Lizzy. Teasing her, I thought. "Go away!" her child's voice shrilled, and she threw all her flowers at him. He ducked and laughed.

"Willy, you fetch the rake and go turn that next field," Tom called out to him.

Willy acted like he hadn't heard for a moment, but I knew he had. If he didn't do what Tom told him to, his father would learn of it at the end of the day. And then there would be extra work; more wood to split maybe, or something messy to do, like cleaning out horse stalls. He hated taking orders from Tom. "Why don't you leave me in charge?" he had asked his father sulkily, last week. "Because you're not fit for it," his father had replied brusquely. That wasn't entirely true; Willy knew what needed doing around this place as well as anybody. But it *was* true that he was better at getting out of work than he was at doing it. Sometimes I had seen him hit the horses, which would have made his father roar with rage.

Finally Willy ambled off in the direction of the barn, muttering to himself. When he left the field, peace descended over me. There was a kind of rhythm I could get into when I was pitching hay. I could think my own thoughts and let my body take care of the work by itself.

I began to think about my birthday, which was today, July 12, 1910. I was fourteen. I decided that maybe, after I got through in this field and went up to the house to make supper, I'd bake myself a cake. It was for sure that no one else around here would make it for me. The hens were laying well, so I'd use a recipe with lots of fresh eggs. I'd beat it light and fluffy. And late in the summer evening, when all the chores were done and Willy had gone off fishing, Lizzy and I would sit on the verandah steps and eat cake and wish on the first star.

Well, there was lots to wish for. For a start, I could ask for a dress that fit. But that wasn't a priority. I could wish that Matthew Howard, who owned this farm, would be in a good mood when I went to negotiate my first wages with him tonight. And I could wish that Kathleen Howard, his wife, would get out of her rocking chair in the parlor and do some work around the house and look after her little daughter, Lizzy. That way I wouldn't be expected to be in five places at once. Washing clothes, heating flat irons, lugging kindling, pouring pig slop, hoeing garden weeds, stirring jam, mending socks, baking bread. Sweating in the fields at planting and harvest — anything, in fact, that Matthew Howard decided I should be busy with.

Or, let's see . . . I could wish that I wouldn't keep dreaming about that girl with the red hair over and over again. That girl I had left behind six years ago, and who looked just like me. Crazy dream. What was she trying to say through the wet glass, anyway? And why did the dream always make me feel so sad? Well, I knew the answer to that, but I didn't want to think about it.

"Watch yourself, Maggie," Tom drawled as he climbed onto the wagon. I stepped back and he chirruped to the horses. They leaned into the traces slowly and dozily, as if their thoughts were somewhere else. The wagon lurched forward, creaking, and moved further down the long swathe of hay. "Whoa now," Tom said. He was good with the horses. They trusted his quiet voice and the easy way his limbs moved. When the wagon was at a standstill again, Tom climbed onto the load of hay we'd pitched up. He began to spread it flat with his fork, trampling it down with his feet.

I straightened my stiff back and looked around. The Howards' farm, where I had lived now for six years, was situated on a long slope of rolling land. There were sixty acres of fields and cedar bush, enclosed by staggering snake fences. I knew almost every corner of it: where to find wild strawberries and trailing black raspberries, where the cows liked to shelter from the north wind, where to pick elderflowers to dry for winter tea. A half mile from the hay field, at the bottom of the slope, the waters of Chemong Lake glittered silver in the sunlight. Behind me, at the top of the slope, stood the square brick farmhouse, the big barn, the driving shed, the woodshed, the hog pen, and the chicken coop. Around the house, and on either side of the gravel drive, maple trees cast soft pools of shade.

The drive went out to the road, and the road led south four miles to the village of Bridgenorth, where we went to collect the mail, or buy supplies, or get horses shod. Not that I went along on these expeditions very often. Mostly Matthew Howard went, driving his fine team of buggy horses. He was there right now, taking his great draught mare, the Clydesdale with the white feathered feet, to visit a stallion.

Horses were more important around this farm than people; I'd figured that out pretty soon. Especially when the horses won blue ribbons at the Peterborough

Industrial Exhibition, like Matthew's horses did every year. Peterborough was further south than Bridgenorth, a bustling town full of churches and shops and hotels. I had arrived there by train six years ago, with only my trunk and my terror. I had stayed a few days at Hazelbrae, the Barnardo house, before being sent to this farm.

I took a deep breath. Popcorn clouds drifted above the hills on the far shores of the lake. Swallows skimmed over the hay field, catching mosquitoes. After all these years, I was happy to be in this country. I had learned to love the space, the sweeping land that was so green this month, the big sky, the generous sun. I loved the poplar trees, standing between me and the lake, their leaves fluttering in the slightest breeze.

While I stood there, breathing it all in, Lizzy came trotting across the stubble to me. "I felled off the rock," she said with a wobble in her voice. Her mouth turned down at the corners. "Kiss it," she commanded.

I kissed the air over the scratch on her knee. "Want to ride on the wagon?"

She nodded and I hoisted her up. She was getting heavy for a four year old. "Stay away from the sides or you'll slip off," I told her. "And don't get in the way of us pitching."

She climbed to the middle of the hay and began to make a nest. "Now, Lily, you sit here," she told her friend, the imaginary one who was always following her around.

I went back to my raking and my own thoughts. What else could I wish for? Oh yes, that I wasn't too old to go to school now that I had turned fourteen. It would be sad not to see Miss Hooper, my teacher, much anymore. Her smile always made me feel better on days when I got to school with hands so cold my head hurt, and on days when Willy was getting to me, and on days when I was tired of being nobody's child. She always noticed how I was feeling about things. Most importantly, Miss Hooper had given me my first flower seeds, and my first little rooted plants. Without her, I might never have found out about my green thumbs, and how much I loved flowers. It was thanks to Miss Hooper that I had my own special place on the farm: the garden along one side of the house, which Tom had helped me enclose in a picket fence.

I would miss some of the girls from school too, like Mae Beth who lived on the farm a mile down the road. Mae Beth's mother decorated her dresses with ricrac that she sewed on by hand, and sometimes she embroidered flowers on the collars of Mae Beth's blouses. Every fall, Mae Beth had new boots to wear; *brand* new, not hand-me-downs. Mae Beth's mother gave us cocoa after school, and had shown me how to make sponge cake. Of course, I could still go and visit there, if I had the time.

What I liked doing best at Mae Beth's house was singing, while her mother played the organ and Mae Beth's two fine older brothers and two smaller sisters joined in. Then Mae Beth and I would stand shoulder to shoulder and sing until we felt weak. She always said I had the best voice of anyone, but maybe that was because she was my friend. Although it's true that, in the fishing town where I came from, the singing in the chapels on Sunday would send chills down your back, it was so beautiful. And the fishermen used to sing, hauling out their nets to dry on the harbor wall. And my father used to sing, carrying me along the beaches on his shoulders on Sunday afternoons. But that was a long time ago.

But now, on my fourteenth birthday, the real thing to wish for was good wages, I decided. And for that I needed Matthew Howard in a good mood. Maybe I would give him some of my sponge cake first. Though that shouldn't have been necessary. Lord knows, I worked hard enough around here, even though the Barnardo Society, who looked after orphans like me, was sending the Howards five dollars a month to help with my food and clothes. Now that I was fourteen, this money would stop arriving.

With a shriek, Lizzy slipped off the side of the wagon and landed with a thump at my feet. She was sobbing when I picked her up. Her fine, curly hair, yellow as buttermilk, was full of dust from the hay. I tried to dry her eyes on the hem of my dress, but she kept crying fresh tears.

"What's the matter?" I asked.

"It's Lily — she's still . . . up there — and she can't get do-o-o-wn," howled Lizzy.

I sighed and walked to the wagon and held out my arms. "Now you jump down, Lily," I said. Lizzy's tears and hiccups stopped. "Lizzy, you run home and fetch us a drink," I suggested. "In the icebox, there's a pitcher of barley water. You carry it out here for us."

"Can Lily come?" she asked.

"For heaven's sake! Take whoever you want," I replied. That Lizzy was enough to drive me crazy, with her invisible friends and her scratches and her legs that got tired so fast I always ended up carrying her.

Now she nodded and trudged away over the field. Soon she was just a dot, moving along the side of the house to the verandah. I ran my tongue around my dry mouth and bent my sweating back over the hay fork again. Stoop, jab, toss. Stoop, jab, toss. My skin itched with pieces of hay. My arms were scratched and turning brown where I'd rolled my long sleeves up. My mouth grew dryer and dryer. Where was that pesky child? I shaded my eyes and looked towards the house, but there was no sign of her. Tom moved the wagon forward again. Faintly, from the next field, came the sound of Willy whistling as he drove the rake up and down, its long curved teeth turning the hay over to dry evenly. I felt like I'd been working in the fields forever.

I glanced at Tom. His white shirt was dark with sweat between his suspenders. He wasn't a talkative man, but if you spoke to him he always answered. I wondered what he thought about hour after hour, tossing hay and brushing horses, milking cows, and hauling stumps and stones out of the ground.

"Do you like farm work?" I asked Tom.

"Beats lumber camps," he said. "'Course, it don't pay too good. Not like some town jobs maybe. If I had a town job, I could get some of that stuff from the Hudson's Bay catalogue."

I knew what stuff he wanted. I'd seen him at night, sitting on a pail in the barn, with the Hudson's Bay catalogue spread out on top of another pail. He pored over the pages by lantern light, running his index finger along the fine print, breathing heavily over pictures of shotguns, fishing lures, fancy saddles, men's overcoats with fur collars. And once when I snuck up on him, he was looking at ladies' chemises. Mae Beth and I liked looking at the catalogue, too. Only we were interested in hats heaped with ostrich feathers, and shoes with rows of buttons, and Persian lamb coats, and sometimes we looked at the couches and the linoleum and the carpets and pretended we were furnishing a new house.

"So what kind of jobs could a girl do in town?" I asked Tom.

He tossed hay for a few minutes before answering. "Well, there's lots of shops to work in," he said thoughtfully. "And then there's fancy houses with maids to keep them clean and cooks to put the meals on the table. But if that's what you're after, you're better to go to Toronto where the rich folks live."

Toronto! This was a city. It was marked on the pale green map of Ontario that Miss Hooper had pinned to the wall, right next to the blackboard. Toronto sat on the shores of the huge Lake Ontario, over ninety miles southwest of the farm. I wondered if I could really get a job there that would pay well, better than farm work. Maybe I could work for a seamstress, bent over a fancy new Singer machine with gleaming black and gold paint. I would sew long straight rows of stitches in wonderful satins and velvets. A ripple of excitement shivered through me. Now that I was fourteen, maybe it was time to take charge of my life. Maybe I didn't always need to be fitting into other folks' plans for me. Fourteen was almost grown up.

I tried to imagine myself going to Toronto. I'd have to run away, since the Barnardo Society considered me their ward until I was twenty-one. That was a long time to wait for my independence. *Run away*. Why not? Again, a shiver of excitement went through me. I turned my face away from Tom, so that he wouldn't notice my expression. Maybe with a city job I could save enough money to go back where I came from. I could go and find that other girl, the one in my dream, who was turning fourteen today too. I was never going to have any peace until she and I had sorted out some things between us.

"Here comes that Lizzy," Tom said.

"And about time." I shaded my eyes and watched her cross the field, staggering slightly with the weight of the pitcher clasped against her chest. As she got closer, I could see how the barley water had slopped over the rim, making wet splotches on her dress.

I poured a drink for each of us into tin cups. Nothing ever tasted as good as cold barley water when I was working in the fields. I felt like drinking the whole pitcherful, but Tom always said that more than one cup of something so cold would give a person the stomachache. So I drank my one cup slowly, making the pleasure last. Then I sent Lizzy to put the pitcher safe in the shade, under the chokecherry trees growing by the fence line.

Just as she wandered away, I heard the faint sound of horses trotting. After a minute, I could see the buggy turn in from the road and come flashing up the drive between the maple trees. Matthew Howard was home again. I hoped he was in a good mood.

Run away, said a little voice in my head again. You could run away.

CHAPTER
TWO

I trudged behind the cows as they headed to the barn for the evening milking. Cedar trees cast long, fuzzy shadows. The lake was a dull sheet, and over the western hills the sky glowed pink as rose petals. The cows swayed ahead of me like loaded ships, their pale udders swinging against their hind legs. Rough brown and white coats gleamed over jutting hip bones. I slapped at mosquitoes humming around my throat and ankles while the farm dog, trailing beside me, snapped at flies. My feet were bare in the lush July grass; I was careful to avoid cow pats and poison ivy, with its three joined leaves. The brown-eyed susans were in bud, and blue devil flowers were like pools of water in the field. I picked long-stemmed hawkweed flowers and braided them into bracelets for my wrists. Once, I hadn't known the names of any of these wild plants.

When I first came to the farm as an eight year old, I knew all about water: neap tides, rip tides, ebb tides. I could name seven different kinds of seashells. I could recognize fish by the color of their scales and the shapes of their sleek bodies: mackerel, haddock, herring, pil-chard, plaice, and fairmaid. But none of this mattered on a farm. Here, I was ignorant. I hadn't even known how to fetch the cows home for milking. "What are you — daft?" Willy would ask. "You're an idiot," he would say. "Don't you know anything?" And I had stuck out my chin and figured I would learn so fast that he would have to take back all his hard words. I did, too.

I learned the names of all the plants on the farm, the names of the birds and what their songs sounded like. I learned how to drive the cows out from under the cedars with a stick in one hand; and what a broody hen was; and how to care for pigs. There was nothing left around the farm that Willy could torment me about. But he still didn't know any of the things I carried hidden in me: about lighthouses and how to clean crabs. It was those things that made me different.

When the cows reached the barnyard, they plodded across the dried mud and filed through the open door of the cow shed. I didn't follow them, because Tom was doing the milking. Willy was up on the barn's main floor, forking the last load of hay off the wagon. I turned towards the house, where Lizzy was supposed to be playing, and then I noticed Mae Beth walking up the driveway. She waved and I waved back. When we met, under a maple tree, she gave me quick hug.

"What are you doing here?" I asked in surprise.

Her mischievous smile created a dimple in each cheek. "Happy birthday, Maggie," she said warmly, and squeezed a small packet, wrapped in brown paper, into my hand. "Open it," she said, flicking her curly yellow bangs. Like her mother, Mae Beth always looked soapy clean, and happy.

The parcel was wrapped with string and I untied the bow slowly, making the moment last. I knew it was the only present I would get, and that Mae Beth had walked a mile to give it to me. I forgot all about the hayseeds stuck everywhere on me, itching and prickling. The paper unrolled, and there lay a long piece of crocheted lace.

"I made it for you," she said. "I thought you could stitch it onto a dress."

"Oh, Mae Beth," I said with a sigh of pleasure. "Thanks for —" I was going to say thanks for the lace, but that didn't seem like enough. I started over again.

"Thanks for all the singing," was what I said, and I think she knew what I meant.

"What's it like, being fourteen?" she asked, because she was six months younger than me.

"Scary," I replied. "Grown up. I have to ask for my wages tonight." My stomach surprised me by giving a lurch as I spoke.

"Oh, Maggie," she said, "you know you'll be okay. Mother says you're a perfect example of a person using hard work and brains to leave the past behind and get on with living life."

I pushed a stone around with one big toe. Maybe I had tried to leave the past behind, but it was still following me. Mae Beth's mother didn't know about my dreams.

"It's funny to think there won't be any more school,"
I said.

"You won't miss it, will you?"

"Well, some parts. Like Miss Hooper and the Christmas play and the spring garden contest. And studying at
your house. And having people to talk to."

"Well, that was a mixed blessing," said Mae Beth,
wrinkling her nose.

I had to laugh. "I won't miss some of those kids."

"I should think not. Remember how you got teased
when you first arrived?" Mae Beth asked.

I nodded. "Calling me a Home child and a slum child,
and trying to copy my accent. There wasn't anyone else
like me."

"And making fun because you didn't know the capital
cities in Canada. And throwing sticks at you, until
Harold beat them all up. Mother didn't know what had
got into him." Mae Beth giggled.

"You and Harold saved me," I said thoughtfully. After
Mae Beth had linked her arm through mine one
lunchtime, and chose me for her friend, things changed
for the better at school. Her brother Harold was broad
shouldered and tall. He carried wood into the classroom
in winter, and he knew lumbermen by name. Walking
home along the dirt roads, he had picked a fight with
everyone who teased me. After that, they left me alone,
except for the small boys who sometimes stuck their
tongues out. Which didn't matter to me.

Now I swallowed heavily. Those days were over.

There would be no more lessons in history and geography, which I was good at. No more lining up along a
crack in the floorboards and spelling out loud. No more
crazy snowball fights at lunch recess, and no more long
walks down dirt roads, with Mae Beth chattering beside
me as we swing our lunch pails. Now there was only
work, and Willy's teasing, and Lizzy's neediness.

"What's wrong?" Mae Beth asked, but I didn't know
how to tell her about it all. Things were different on her
farm — people coming and going, trips to church teas
and hymn sings and sailing regattas on the lake.

"I'm just tired. We've been in the fields all day and
now I've got to get supper. And . . . I don't know . . . I
have to decide things."

"What do you mean?"

"Well, like if I want to work on a farm the rest of my
life. Or what I'm going to do. I mean, this isn't really my
home."

Mae Beth stared. I could tell she had never thought
about the future like this. It was different for her; she was
part of a family. She didn't have to get wages just to buy
herself clothes, or to earn the food she ate.

"Well, maybe one day some young man will come
along and marry you and you'll have a farm of your own,"
Mae Beth suggested at last.

I shrugged. I wanted to ask if she thought I should
run away, and to tell her about the girl with red hair
who I had to find. But before I could ask, Mae Beth
spoke again.

"Maybe Harold will marry you," she teased.

"Mae Beth!" I protested, flushing. I jerked so hard on the hawkweed flowers that they broke and fell from my wrist. It was time to change the subject. "Can you come in?" I asked.

Mae Beth shook her head. "I told mother I'd be right back to can rhubarb sauce. Can you come over some time?"

"Maybe when the hay is in," I replied.

"Oh, and I nearly forgot — the circus is coming to Peterborough next week. We'll take two buggies and Mother says you're welcome to ride with me and Minnie and Harold. Can you come?"

I didn't know what to say, because if I started working for wages, I might not be able to take time off. "I'll ask," I said with a smile. But I knew I looked anxious. Mae Beth hugged me goodbye, and I watched her walking away up the drive, her jaunty step making the ruffles on her skirt flounce and swing. The pointed toes of her boots twinkled in the light. She waved when she reached the road, and then I headed back to make supper, the length of lace deep in my pocket.

The fields were in shadow now, but the Howards' square brick house, on top of its hill, caught the last rays of sun. The front door was closest to the drive, but I went past it and around to the west side of the house. Here the red bricks were glowing and warm in the sunlight. There was a verandah running along this wall, with a view out over the lake and the hills. The four posts, which held up the verandah roof, gleamed white. Under the eaves, the carved gingerbread trim was as pale as icing sugar.

I paused by the verandah steps and took a look at my flower garden. The picket fence around it was unpainted, and had been built one winter using rough wood. Tom had found two hinges in the driving shed, and he'd built a little gate and nailed the hinges onto it. Inside the fence, my plants were growing thick and bushy and brilliant green. Morning glory vines climbed up the strings I had stretched for them. Their heart-shaped leaves made a curtain across the verandah. Marigold plants were brilliant with orange and yellow flowers. Hollyhocks stretched upwards, tall and stiff as pokers. Cosmos had feathery foliage and nasturtiums hugged the ground. I thought I could almost feel the plants' contentment as the evening sun warmed them. It was what I was most proud of in my life, my garden.

With a guilty start, I noticed Matthew Howard come out of the driving shed and cross the yard to the barn. I knew I had better quit daydreaming and get supper ready. The smell of baked beans, drifting down the verandah steps, made my stomach rumble. Before going in, I ran to the garden and picked some radishes and some small, tender lettuce. There wasn't time to worry about shelling peas. Then I climbed the verandah steps, crossed the bare floorboards and opened the screen door.

The house was dim and warm and still. Slanting squares of light fell across the worn linoleum pattern on the kitchen floor. Lizzy's face was a pale oval beneath the heavy, scrubbed wood of the table. She had an old piece of quilt spread over one knee. I'd been using it for a rag.

"Hungry," she said as soon as I walked in. "Maggie, I'm hungry."

"You're always hungry. What are you doing down there?"

"Me 'n Lily are having a quilting bee. Can you get some 'fread?" she lisped.

"Not just now," I said with a sigh. My voice had a flat, tired sound.

I had left the beans simmering that morning in an iron pot on the wood stove. Now I lifted the lid and gave them a stir. They were soft and so was the knuckle of ham in the middle of the pot. I ran out for the wood that was stacked by the door. I slid another hunk of dry elm into the firebox, and blew on the embers. Ash whirled into my face and I slammed the door shut with a clang. Then I fetched water from the pump outside the door, washed my hands, and scooped cornmeal from an enamel bin to make johnnycake with. Quickly I mixed the dough, scooped it into a pan, and slid the pan into the oven. By the time the men came in, the johnnycake would be ready to serve with the beans.

I washed the dough from my hands, stepped outside and flung the dirty water onto the grass, then ran the pump to fill the basin again. I used this water to wash the lettuce and radishes, and then I arranged them on a plate, and began to set the table. The sunlight had gone now and the room was dusky. I lit the oil lamp on its wall bracket, and suddenly my shadow flickered across the black iron stove and the braided rug beside the table.

Pots gleamed on their hooks, and bunches of drying herbs hung motionless. I sat down on a wooden chair and thought about making a sponge cake. My back ached, my arms ached. My face was stretched tight and hot with sun. I was too tired to care about the cake. It didn't seem to matter anymore. Besides, I had Mae Beth's lace. Every time I thought of her walking over to give it to me, I felt a smile pulling at the corners of my mouth.

"Maggie, are you there? Maggie?"

I sighed and forgot about the lace. Without a word I got up and went down the hall to the parlor, feeling sorry for myself.

"I'm here," I said.

The room was airless and dim. My bare toes curled over the edge of the dark red carpet that began where I stood in the doorway. The carpet stretched right across to the opposite wall, where olive green wallpaper was decorated with dark red roses. Silhouetted against the window, Kathleen Howard swayed to and fro in her rocking chair. To and fro. To and fro. With each rock, the chair gave a squeak so small that it was only a whisper of sound.

"Supper's almost ready," I said. "Do you want the lamp lit in here?"

"No," she replied in her thin, light voice. "I'm looking out."

I came and stood by her chair, which faced the window. The hills were dark purple now and the lake was black. A wisp of cloud, high up, gleamed bright as a fish scale and there was a slender crescent moon.

"I want to go and see the children," she said suddenly. My heart sank. "We're busy in the hay," I replied but she ignored me.

"Tomorrow," she said. "You'll come with me, Maggie."

"There's raspberries to pick, and the corn needs hoeing, and the hay's not finished," I told her. When I thought about all the work, I felt hot in my chest. Then the anger crawled up my throat and filled my mouth. I clenched my teeth. It was fine for her, sitting there day after day, rocking and staring into space, seeing things no one else could see. Meanwhile, everyone's clothes got dirty and ripped, and the milk stood warm in the cans, waiting to be churned and salted and packed into butter boxes. I didn't have time to get in the buggy and drive away to look at tombstones.

"Kathleen —" I began boldly, but she waved my words away with one of her slender, dry hands.

"Is there supper?" she asked. "I think I could eat some tonight." And she rose from her chair, her dress hanging limply against her fine bones. When she followed me into the light of the kitchen, I thought of how everything about her looked tired: her flat sandy hair and her pale blue eyes and her thin arms. Which was funny, when you thought about how much of the work I did for her.

Just as she sat down, the screen door swung open and Matthew Howard strode in. His huge shadow leapt across the floor, dark as his thick beard and thick hair. Dark as a bear. He scraped out a chair and shoved his long legs and his boots under the table. There was a sudden whimper.

I stooped down and hauled Lizzy out, her piece of rag quilt clenched in one chubby fist. She was half asleep and a dead weight. She rubbed the back of her hand across her nose and her scrunched-up eyes, and began to howl.

"Hush, hush," I soothed her. "It's supper time. Hush." I put a spoon into her hand and propped her up in a chair.

Willy came in from outside, and pushed his face close to Lizzy's. "Shut up your noise," he said crossly, then slid into a chair when his father glanced at him. Tom came in quietly, as I lifted the bean pot into the center of the table. When we were all seated, Mr. Howard carved up the johnnycake and ladled out the beans. The ladle's thin handle disappeared into his huge hand, with its black hairs on the back of each finger.

I shoveled beans into my mouth. They were salty and good. The cake was sweet and good, too. I chewed and swallowed automatically, like a cow chewing the cud, because I was too exhausted to enjoy my own cooking. My body slumped in the chair, too tired to hold itself straight. After the next swallow, I thought, I will ask Mr. Howard if I can talk to him later. My throat tightened up. I spooned more beans into my mouth. I would ask him after this mouthful. I swallowed and spooned in more beans. I couldn't believe that speaking could be so difficult. I opened my mouth. Tom glanced at me expectantly and I closed it again and bent my face over my food. The lamp hissed. Spoons scraped on plates. Lizzy smacked her lips as she chewed. I swallowed past a lump in my throat, and opened my mouth to try speaking again. I took a breath.

"I'm going to see the children," Kathleen said.

Matthew glanced at her, an unreadable look. "You're wasting your time."

"Maggie's coming with me," she said. Her mouth closed around the words like water around a stone.

There was a moment's heavy silence. Willy squinted at his plate. Tom cleared his throat.

"Maggie's got work to do," Matthew said. He made it sound like an order.

"Maggie is coming to drive the buggy. I can't go alone," Kathleen replied.

Silence.

And then, *crash!* Cutlery skittered and jumped as Matthew's fist hit the table. "You're wasting your time," he roared. "There's nothing you can do for them now!"

I flinched and then willed myself to be very still. Lizzy's eyes stretched huge. Her mouth puckered and hastily I pushed a piece of lettuce into her hand. Don't you dare cry again, I thought. Making more trouble when there's enough here already.

Kathleen hadn't jumped. She stared at her husband, one of those looks that went right through you and out the other side. Her face was smooth and blank in the flickering light, and even when Lizzy began to cry again I knew Kathleen wasn't listening. She was off in her own world, the one only she could see. I scooped Lizzy into my arms and carried her slowly up the dark, creaking stairs. I knew that in the morning Tom would hitch up the team and I would climb into the buggy beside

Kathleen. I knew she would want flowers from my garden, to lay under the headstones.

I knew I wasn't going to ask Matthew Howard about wages tonight.

Lizzy slept in the smallest room. I dropped her onto her bed, and fumbled for the candle I had left on the one piece of furniture, a low chest of drawers. The match rasped in the dark. The candle flame flickered and grew tall. I pulled Lizzy's floppy arms out of her dress, and smoothed her nightgown over her head. It was getting too small. Her knees were chubby and dimpled at the hem. When I pulled the light summer blanket up to her chin, her arms clung around my neck.

"Let go, you're hurting my back," I told her.

"Tell me a story," she mumbled.

"Not tonight."

"Why, Maggie? Tell me a story. A little one." Her lower lip trembled ominously.

"No, I'm too tired."

"Tell about the giant on the mountain."

"Lizzy, you just lie down and be quiet and go to sleep," I snapped. "Good night and don't let the bugs bite," I said as I closed the door.

My own room was right beside Lizzy's and I carried the candle into it. The door creaked behind me. First thing I did was slide the bolt across. Then I sagged against the door, numb with tiredness.

Why did Lizzy always need me so much? She was eating me alive, with her crying and her requests for songs and stories and piggyback rides. Why did I have to

be like a mother when I wasn't even a grownup yet? It
didn't seem fair. I didn't want to be mean to Lizzy but
I couldn't tell her a story about Cornish giants tonight.
I just couldn't; I didn't have the strength.

Being alone in my room was a relief. The room was
almost as empty as Lizzy's, but I loved it because it
was the only place I could be private. My clothes were
all in the wardrobe, my petticoats and hose, my cotton
dresses for summer and the flannelette ones for winter.
The wardrobe had an oval mirror on its door, with a
crack down the middle that hinted at some past accident
or act of violence. Beside the wardrobe stood my trunk,
the one thing that was really mine. I loved it because of
this. Also, I loved it because of the distance it had
traveled with me to this small bedroom with faded paint
and scuffed pine floor. Inside my trunk I kept my few,
treasured possessions: the Bible with its thick black
cover embossed with gold lettering, a copy of *Pilgrim's
Progress*, a prayer book with pages as thin as petals.
Three seashells from a beach in another country.

Before I pulled off my clothes, I remembered the lace.
I took it from my pocket and admired it. It made the
fabric of my dress look even worse than usual, so rough
and faded. Then I laid the lace in the trunk, beside my
seashells, and closed the lid again. Once I had my nightie
on, I blew out the candle and, sitting on the hard edge of
my bed, wondered who was going to clean up the supper
in the kitchen. Not that I cared. The dirty dishes,
smeared with beans, could sit on the table overnight, as
far as I was concerned. Or Willy could take care of them,

I thought sourly. No chance of that happening. No one would yell at him if the food went stale in the warm air; it was my name they would holler. But I wasn't going back down tonight. I tried to imagine the scene in the kitchen — who was still eating, who was talking, if anyone would remember to close the damper on the wood stove. But I couldn't see any of it clearly.

I was seeing the red haired girl instead, the one in my dreams. Was she never going to leave me alone? I would have to go and find her, and ask her why they had all loved her more than they loved me. Why they had kept her and sent me away, far away, across the ocean, to this farm in another country, another world. With only my anger and my own tough, skinny strength to keep me going.

But if I couldn't get good wages, how could I save up enough to go back and find her? *Run away*, I thought again, but no excitement shivered through me this time. Run away into the dark, and the sound of coyotes yipping? Run away with no money and no map? Leave behind my trunk? I would have to be crazy. And what did I know about a city girl's work and a city girl's wages? I was trapped here.

I sighed and went to the window to draw the curtains against the glimmer of the moon and the stars shining in the lake. It was water that had brought trouble to this family. The barn roof was black and straight against the sky. I pulled the edges of cotton cloth smoothly together over the glass, but a breath of air puffed them open. The smell of dry earth and growing things came into my room.

When I lay down, all the bones in my body went as soft as a starfish. I shut my eyes like curtains, but memories came into my mind anyway: a high tide of sadness, a girl I only sometimes loved, the faces of my parents.

CHAPTER
THREE

Thomasina and I always shared the top bunk. Even though it was narrow, neither of us ever rolled out. We slept with our warm arms and legs tangled together, our bony knees and sharp elbows interlocked. When I woke with golden red hair in my mouth or across my eyes, it was sometimes my own but sometimes hers. The color was identical, the way the color of our freckles was identical, and the color and shape of our eyes. We were twins; she was half of me.

One November night, when we were six years old, a northeast gale blew over Cornwall, the part of England where we lived. Black seas churned against rocks; pale foam flew from the tops of the waves. Leaves and branches, seaweed, torn sails, broken rope, and seagulls were hurled across the roaring dark. In St. Ives, our fishing town, slates crashed from rooftops and shattered on cobblestones below.

Mother sat by the range and held a wool sock on her belly, darning it. Her belly was a smooth curve; there was a baby inside it. Sometimes Thomasina and I flattened our palms there and felt the baby's feet sliding around. Mother's needle flashed in the glow from the fire. Coals shifted in the grate.

Thomasina and I climbed the stairs and lay in our top bunk. We listened to Mother singing something from chapel about the Lord calming the winds of heaven and holding the waves in His hand. Wind cried under the eaves.

Bang! Bang!

"What is it?" Thomasina whispered, but I was already wriggling away from her. I landed like a cat and rushed downstairs with Thomasina at my heels. We pressed our faces to the window overlooking the harbor.

Bang! The lights exploded upwards, pink arcs of brilliance against the racing clouds. Thomasina pushed against my arm. "What is it?" she asked more loudly.

"Tez the flares," Mother said behind us. "Some poor chaps es in trouble. The lifeboat will be putting out."

"Father?" I asked.

"'Es, yer father," she confirmed.

Thomasina and I were proud of Father, how he could heft us high onto his wide shoulders and carry us along the beach. How his great voice rolled out over the women's hats in chapel. We liked to press our noses to his fisherman's smocks and jerseys, smelling the tar, pipe smoke, salt. We loved it when the lifeboat went out to practice on blue winter afternoons, pushing its bows into the swells, with our father telling the men what to do in his warm, rough voice. He was the coxswain. He saved lives. He knew the sea like another person; its moods, its meanings.

I pressed my face to the glass. Against my arm I could feel the goosebumps on Thomasina's skin. Men and lanterns rushed past the window, going downhill to the harbor and the lifeboat house. Father would be there already; he'd been telling stories at the Fisherman's Lodge. The fire sank lower. Thomasina shivered.

"Skeddadle back to bed," Mother told us.

In the bunk, we wrapped our cold arms and legs together. Thomasina's soft breathing stirred over my face. Wind shrieked and cried under the eaves and Mother stood in the window although there was nothing to see. When I was warm, I slept.

In the morning, Thomasina and I pulled on our smocks and went down to the harbor, hanging onto Mother's hands. The seas were breaking over the harbor wall in white sheets. A knot of figures leaned into the wind. The lifeboat house was empty. All day, people came to our house and drank tea. Even at low tide, the waves came high up the beach. Thomasina and I played in the alleys, where there was shelter.

The wind blew for three days and on the third day pieces of the lifeboat, and the bodies of two men, washed up on the rocks at Hawk's Point. The flag went to half-mast at the Fisherman's Lodge. Mother put away the sock she had been darning for three days, emptied the teapot, pinned her hat over her long brown hair, and took Thomasina and me by the hand. Father was dead. The sea had taken him.

In chapel, the minister prayed for the souls of brave

men who laid down their lives in the service of others. Thomasina and I pressed our legs against each other on the hard bench. We held hands with white knuckles. We were as joined, and as still, as one lump of stone.

◇ ◇

Life went on. Spring came, with gulls nesting on the rooftops of St. Ives. Children and dogs ran on the beach. The pilchard seiners went out looking for fish. The men complained that the fish were hard to find this year. Nets hung empty, dry and mended along the harbor wall.

One afternoon, when Thomasina and I came out from school, our uncle met us in the street. He bent his tall, wide body down to us. We liked him because — although he was Mother's brother — he reminded us of Father. He had the same thick, curling beard and he was a fisherman and he smelled the way Father had smelled.

"Eh, me dear maids," he said softly to us. "You're to come 'ome with me."

Our hands disappeared into his huge callused grasp, and we trotted beside his long legs, trying to keep up over cobbles slimy with fish and seagull droppings. I pretended his legs were Father's legs, and that his warm hands were Father's hands. For a moment, I was almost happy. I could feel the same thing in Thomasina.

Uncle Jan's house was a narrow stone cottage like our own. We followed him through the low doorway into a dark kitchen full of commotion.

"Mother, tez my bun!"

"Aw! Eddent hers! Her n' Sally had two already!"

shrieked a small boy. His sister pushed him; he slapped back.

Their mother, a woman with arms as massive as hams, pulled my fighting cousins apart and shoved them out the door. "Git out, the lot of you heathens!" she shouted. Bodies pushed past us, six of them, all cousins. In the sudden silence, my aunt folded her red, rough arms over her great chest and stared at Thomasina and me with cool gray eyes. "You children can stay 'ere tonight," she stated. "Yer mawther's 'aving the baby."

Thomasina was stiff against my arm, like an old stick on the beach. We both nodded and then we went out to play in the narrow streets, with the cousins. They were wild and ragged. In summer, the boys jumped naked off the harbor wall into the incoming tide. They chased cats and threw stones and teased. "Yah, Maggie Magpie!" they yelled at me. "Can't catch me!" And when I chased them they led me down a dead-end alley and turned on me and knocked me to the ground. Thomasina came to my defense, her fists striking out blindly. The boys shrieked with laughter. "Tommie can fight!" they yelled. "Tommie can fight like a Turk. Ow, ow, we're skeered!" They rushed us, and we put our backs against the wall and faced them, shoulder to shoulder, sharp chins lifted. By bedtime, we had scraped knees and bruised elbows. Under the blankets, we curled up tight and didn't say anything about Mother.

Uncle Jan came for us after school the next day, too. He took our hands silently. His eyes were red and his mouth had a pinched look. I remembered once when

Father had a toothache. "Do your teeth hurt, Uncle Jan?" I asked.

He looked as if he didn't understand. Then he heaved a huge gusting sigh. "No, nawthing wrong with my teeth," he said. But he didn't smile to show them to me and he didn't say anything else all the way to his house.

That night, the kitchen was empty, except for our aunt. "Be gentle with en," Uncle Jan told her. "I'm away to the boat." He took his coat from behind the door and went out. I could hear his seaboots going downhill over the cobbles.

"Set down," our aunt said.

We sat side by side, on stools with loose legs, against the black, dull belly of the stove. Our aunt gave us tea in china cups with cracked rims. She folded her freckled, rough arms and stared at us as we drank nervously. Her breathing was loud. Her face was red and rough from working on the beaches; from walking the windy streets, selling fish from the basket on her back.

"Me 'andsomes," she said at last, "yer mawther and the babe es both dead. You'll 'ave to live 'ere with us. Though dear knows 'ow I'm to feed another two hungry mouths." She sighed and knotted her red hands.

We drank in silence. We got up, like one person, and went out behind the harbor wall because the tide was low.

"She's lying!" I yelled. "I hate her! Mother wouldn't go without saying goodbye!"

"She's not lying — it's true," Thomasina said soberly. "It's because Father's gone. He wouldn't have let this happen."

We stared at the water, the faraway white needle of the lighthouse on its black rocks. Lazy swells moved across the bay. When the sun touched the sea, the water glowed brilliant green.

"I hate it," Thomasina said passionately.

I looked, and hated it too. We stood on the wet sand, united by our misery against the deceptive, restless water that had taken away our family. We ran along the sand with our fists clenched, until the sky blurred and our legs ached. We collapsed against the rough stones of the harbor wall and sobbed as if we'd never stop. We smoothed each other's hair. We wiped each other's noses on our own sleeves. We wrapped our arms around each other and were silent. When the tide came sliding in, we let the water come to our ankles before dragging ourselves back to Uncle Jan's house.

We lived there for a year, fighting with our cousins, running wild in the alleys, sitting dazed and uncaring in school with our broken slates and our chilblained hands. We were never apart. We didn't go much to the beaches, because we hated the sea. All we wanted was to be left alone, to escape from our aunt's yelling and scolding, our cousins' taunts, our uncle's mournful eyes. The girl cousins scratched when they fought, but Thomasina and I could take care of each other.

Things were going badly in St. Ives for the pilchard seiners. I heard the men talking about it on the street corners, outside The Sloop, in my uncle's kitchen over a pot of tea. The pilchards had stopped coming. Day after day the huers, who watched for the bright shoals of fish from the headlands and cliffs, saw nothing. No one knew why the fish had stopped coming, why boats and nets and men sat idle. Why children went hungry and there was no money in the downlong houses of St. Ives, where the fishing families lived. One night, when I was awake in bed, I heard my aunt and uncle talking in the kitchen.

"Look at en! Take a good look at en," my aunt said. She had a voice like stones grating on a beach. "Take a look, Jan Trebillcock. Tez the last shilling in this 'ouse yer gawping at. Yer children are in rags. Edn't more'n half a caddie of tea and a heel of bread in the cupboard. Those two children 'ave to go. They're not yourn and yourn are hungry as gannets."

"They're my sister's children," remonstrated my uncle in his soft voice.

"I won't keep en," she said.

"Where will'n go?"

"There's old Mabel Curnow, their father's aunt over to Nancledra. Let 'er feed en for awhile."

I held my breath, but no more was said, and, after a few days, I forgot about what I had heard. It was summer, but I was always cold and hungry. Thomasina and I shared everything, every piece of bread. Once a man in a boat threw us an apple. It was last year's and wrinkled, but we took turns biting it until there were only seeds left. Then we had a contest to see who could spit the seeds furthest.

One night, when Thomasina and I were scrambling up the steep stairs to bed, our aunt came and stood below us. "You children es going away tomorrow, the two of ee," she said. "There's too many mouths in this 'ouse. Pack your belongings."

There wasn't much to pack. In the narrow bedroom we shared with two girl cousins, we took our cloth bags from the wardrobe. We folded our dresses and our aprons. Thomasina had six seashells; she put three in her bag and three in mine.

"Where are we going?" she asked under the blankets.

"To Father's aunt at Nancledra," I told her. "Remember what I heard?"

She nodded; her breathing slowed. We both slept.

My aunt's hard hands shook us awake. "Up, up!" she said. "The pony trap es coming for ee. Git dressed." Her feet clumped back down the stairs.

In the chilly, dim light we fumbled with our clothes. A button fell from Thomasina's dress and rolled across the floor. A girl cousin's arm shot out from under the covers and her fingers curled around the button.

"Give it to me," Thomasina begged. "I have to sew it on."

I crossed the room and stepped on the arm. The fingers uncurled. "Bleddy heathen," the cousin swore at me, but I didn't answer. Thomasina cared about clothes more than I did. She liked to be neat; she would not go to Nancledra with a button missing. Already she had pulled from her bag the tiny sewing kit, with its needles and threads, that our mother had once owned.

"Git a move on, ee great lummox!" my aunt roared up the stairs. "Do I have to come and get ee by the scruffs?"

"Go. Go down," said Thomasina. "I'll catch you up."

I took my bag and went down the bare steps to the

kitchen's dim warmth. The door was standing open and I could see the wheels of a pony trap in the street outside. A breeze wafted in the doorway along with the sound of the pony snorting.

My aunt took hold of the cloth on my back, and steered me through the door. "'Ere she es then," she said to the woman sitting in the trap, and she half lifted me up the steps and onto the seat.

My legs swung. The woman smiled at me; she was the minister's wife from chapel. I remembered her crying into a lace hanky when my mother died. But she wasn't my father's aunt from Nancledra; I didn't understand what was happening.

"Lunch for both of ee," my aunt said briefly, pushing a parcel wrapped in brown paper into my hands.

The paper felt warm, and I could tell from the shape that there were pasties inside. The minister's wife chirruped prettily to the pony and the cart lurched forward. Something terrible and swift ran through my veins. "Wait!" I cried. "Wait! Wait for Thomasina!"

The minister's wife flicked her whip over the pony's chestnut haunches and shook her head as we rattled away over the cobbles. "There's another pony trap coming for her," she explained.

I didn't understand again. I stared backwards. My aunt blocked the cottage doorway, her rough hands on her wide hips. Suddenly I saw Thomasina hurtle against her. My aunt caught her and held her. Thomasina kicked and my aunt turned and pulled her inside the house. For one fraction of time, that lasted all my life, I saw Thomasina's face in the crook of my aunt's arm. The door closed. Then the house was gone, around a corner. The wind from the sea hit us, ruffling the pony's mane. Its hooves rang smartly on the cobbles. I was blinded by sunlight. My blood was cold.

"When is she coming?" I asked.

The minister's wife smiled at me. "As soon as the trap arrives from Nancledra."

"Why can't she come with us?" I persisted, but the minister's wife didn't reply. Outside the chapel she slowed the pony, and the minister came down the steps and swung into the trap. I was squashed small between the two adults.

"Eh, dear maid," he said, fumbling in one pocket. "Here's something for the trip." And he handed me a silver sixpence. I slipped it into my bag. I hoped Thomasina would get one too.

The pony slowed to a walk as we climbed the hill out of St. Ives, but trotted again as we reached the level yard by the railway station. I kept craning my head around, looking for the other pony trap with Thomasina in it. Outside the station building, the minister's wife went in to buy tickets and the minister gave me a humbug to suck on. "Are we going by train to Nancledra?" I asked.

"'Es, going by train," he replied. His face was sad, like the face of Abraham walking up the mountain to sacrifice his son, Isaac. In chapel, the minister's wife had showed us a picture of this. But it had been all right in the end, because God had sent a sheep and Isaac had lived and not died.

I followed the minister's wife onto the train. I carried my bag with the pasties inside it, and she carried a smart traveling case and the tickets. I sat down by the window and pressed my face to the glass. The minister turned the pony and trap around and waved goodbye. Smoke and ashes from the engine drifted past the window. The train trembled.

"We have to wait!" I cried. "We have to wait for Thomasina!" I couldn't see any pony and trap bringing her to the station. Smoke belched past in dark clouds. The coaches lurched. Creaked. Moved forward. The platform slid past, slowly, then faster.

At last, my mind understood what my body had known.

With a yell of panic, I leapt up, but the minister's wife had me by both arms. I kicked her shins. I screamed and sobbed and struggled, but she was a fisherman's daughter like me, and older, and stronger. She held me fast.

As our coach slid past the end of the platform, I saw my uncle Jan running into the station. His long legs ate up the ground, but he was too late. I saw him calling, his mouth a wide "O". He ran to the end of the platform, waving his hat. I lay my face against a black shiny dress and went down into darkness and terror.

They had kept Thomasina, but they were sending me away. This time, it was me who had died.

◇ ◇

The minister's wife, Mrs. Trenoweth, was going to London to visit her sister. It wasn't her fault I was being sent away. She had only agreed to keep me company when my aunt had gone and asked her. She sat stiff and frightened in her shiny black dress, hour after hour, while I cried. The countryside rolled past outside: the bright green hills, the foxgloves swaying their purple bells, the daisies white as drifts of snow. The train lumbered in and out of stations. Passengers climbed on and off, with parcels and bags and shivering dogs and sandwiches wrapped in crackling paper. Mrs. Trenoweth ate one of my aunt's pasties but I refused to eat mine. Whistles shrilled, doors slammed. Smoke flew across fields of grazing cows. Every turn of the wheels, every second, took me further from Thomasina. I died all the way to London, which was dark and confusing, crowded and noisy. I was floating now, grimy, starving, cold. I floated behind Mrs. Trenoweth to a hansom cab that hauled us through congested streets and blowing papers, gas lamps, shouting, horses neighing and snorting, wheels grinding.

Finally we stopped before a tall, wide building and I followed Mrs. Trenoweth's rustling black hem up a flight of steps. She hugged me goodbye. She was sorry for me, I knew, but it didn't matter. It didn't change anything.

"Be a good maid," she told me. "They'll take care of you here. Eh, I'm that sorry about your mother. Dear soul." She pressed her hanky to my face and I smelled the rosewater in it.

"Is Thomasina at Nancledra?" I asked.

"With your father's aunt," she agreed.

Then she was leaving and another woman, with a stiff white apron, led me away down long halls with shining floors, and into a room lined with beds. Hundreds of them, it seemed, all full of girls asleep or pretending. The woman showed me where to wash my face and go to the toilet, then took me to an empty bed, and turned back the coarse sheets. I climbed in and lay rigid in the dark.

If I didn't move a single muscle, I could fool my body that Thomasina was in bed with me. She was there, just an inch away, but I wouldn't reach out and touch her. Not right now. I would let her sleep. I sat up and ate my pasty very quietly; I thought she had eaten hers already. In the morning, I would tell her that it wasn't a good pasty, like the ones Mother made. There was no meat in it, and no salt. When the pasty was gone, I lay down and breathed with my mouth open. The air ran up over my cheek, like it did when Thomasina slept with her face turned towards mine. As long as I kept breathing like this, I couldn't scream.

◇ ◇

This great building full of children, to which Mrs. Trenoweth had delivered me, was called Stepney Causeway. It belonged to a society run by Dr. Barnardo, a man who cared for orphans like me.

I lived there in a fog, a floating mist of despair. Without Thomasina, I was only half alive. In church service, my mouth moved but my voice was silent. I polished floors until they shone, on my knees, with rows of other girls. At mealtimes, at the long tables, I chewed so slowly and carefully that I forgot to swallow. My ears listened to lectures about a country across the ocean, called Canada; a wonderful place full of opportunity where we could make new lives and be a credit to England, our motherland. But my mother was dead, and how could I start a new life when there was only half of me here, in this city of London? When there was only half of me to send away to Canada?

I cried for Thomasina all the time, in my thoughts and in my bones. I cried for her when they gave us our trunks, packed full of hose, dresses, petticoats, aprons, hats, and handkerchiefs. There was also a Bible, *Pilgrim's Progress*, and a hymn book. It was more than I had ever owned, but none of it mattered to me. I cried when they dressed us in identical matching gray dresses, two hundred girls with red coats and soft hats. Each girl wore a tag with her name and a number on it. I cried on the train that took us north, past smoking chimneys and through the grimy back streets of Liverpool to the docks; and as we walked to the great ship.

Our feet thundered on the gangway. The ropes from the ship were wrapped around huge bollards on the dock. We watched the stevedores untie them. The water looked flat from high up on deck, as we leaned against the railing. When the shores of England became a smudge on the horizon, I went to my bunk and pulled the covers over my head.

Why had they sent me away? Why had they kept Thomasina? We were the same. How could they choose? She was a little shorter and a little thinner than me — did they think she would be cheaper to feed? She was neater than me. She liked working in the house. She could stitch a straight seam. Did they think she would suit an old aunt better? Did they think I was wild? Was there something about me, some terrible defect, that I didn't know about? Was it the reason they didn't love me?

And then, the most terrible thought of all: how could Thomasina have let them send me away? Did she know this would happen? Was it the reason she had stayed upstairs, sewing a button? Was she part of their secret plans? Had she agreed to let me go downstairs alone?

I thought of her face in the door, in the crook of my aunt's arm. I felt her anguish. But now I was angry at her. In anger I strode up and down the decks of the ship, glaring at the wrinkled sea. In anger I played games with the other children, throwing my ball too hard and too fast, smashing it into the skittles. Angrily, I snatched for my mug of cocoa before bed, slopping the drink over the rim, dribbling on the floor. I was unloved, unlovable. I would act that way. I glared at the adult passengers when they smiled at me. I refused to talk to the other girls. Standing at the stern of the ship, I watched the ribbon of pale wake unfurling to the horizon. It was the thread that still joined me to England, to Thomasina. I was angry at the spouting whales, the drifting icebergs, the wide river we sailed up one night, the lights of Canada twinkling on the bank. I was furious with the doctor who examined us on the shore, curling back our eyelids painfully.

I hated the Canadian countryside, flashing past the train windows. I ignored the other girls, laughing and playing in the corridors. The girl in the seat by mine smelled of pee; I said I wouldn't sit with her. I sat on the

floor instead, and tripped up the people who passed.
My shoes pinched. I threw one out the train window
and arrived at a town called Peterborough wearing
borrowed shoes three sizes too big. Girls laughed. I stuck
my tongue out.

For three days I fumed in the brick house, called
Hazelbrae, that the mayor of the town had given to
Dr. Barnardo for all his stupid orphans. On the fourth
day, a horse and buggy came for me. They loaded my
trunk. They lifted me in beside a dark, silent man called
Matthew Howard, who drove me north out of town
without speaking to me.

For the first time, I remembered to be afraid. Dusk
came through the billowing, suffocating trees. The
buggy jolted over the rough road. In a swamp, dead trees
leaned stiffly, at odd angles. The dark was full of strange
sounds: howls and yips and rustles. We went on and on
into this alien landscape, where I knew nothing and
nobody. Where I was losing myself with every jolt of the
wheels. Now that I was far from the ocean, the thread
that led back to Thomasina had vanished.

When we arrived at the red house on the hill, I was
no one. Everything that had been me, *Maggie Curnow*,
was gone.

CHAPTER
FOUR

I had stayed awake so long the night before, remembering my parents and Thomasina and how I had come to Canada, that my eyes would hardly open in the morning. When I came down to the kitchen, I was awake just enough to notice that someone had cleaned away the dirty plates from supper. I looked in the enamel basin, but they weren't there. When I opened the cupboard, I saw that they were inside it, stacked and clean. I wondered who had done it.

I put oatmeal into the big pot, added water, and put it on to cook. The wood stove was hot already. It was Willy's job to light it before he went out to help Tom milk the cows each morning. I set the table, then went out to my flower garden.

Dew glimmered on the leaves. I picked nasturtiums, marigolds, and pansies. I held them to my face, and the cool, soft, damp petals fluttered against me like kisses. Even though the sun wasn't up yet, the flowers glowed with color: orange, corn yellow, sand, wine red, the kind of deep purple blue that the sky turns after sunset on summer nights.

I arranged the flowers in three little bunches and tied each one with a long stem of grass. Then I hurried back inside to stir the porridge, and put the flowers in a jar of water.

Breakfast was a silent affair. Tom and Willy arrived smelling like cows and rubbing their eyes. Willy's mouth kept cracking open with huge yawns that made his jaw bones poke close to the surface of his skin. Mr. Howard heaped his bowl to the brim with steaming porridge. Lizzy and Kathleen Howard were both still in bed. While we ate, the cows wandered back to the fields and the sun came up through the maples, a pulsing ball of gold.

Spoons clattered on bowls. After his second helping was finished, Mr. Howard stood up, scraping his chair back. Outside the door, the dog whined. "Willy, you go on tedding that hay you started on yesterday," Matthew Howard ordered. "Tom, you take the mower and cut the last field. But before you do, hitch Blossom to the buggy for Mrs. Howard."

Tom and Willy nodded and left, their boots clumping across the verandah. Matthew Howard turned his heavy gaze on me. Everything about him always seemed heavy: the darkness of his beard; the way his eyes had no light in them; the flat, thick sound of his voice. I stood with two dirty bowls in my hand and waited for him to give me my orders for the day, as he did every morning.

"Maggie, you take Mrs. Howard into Bridgenorth to see the — to visit the cemetery. And here's a list of things you can get at the store. Don't lose the money. Count your change. And don't drive the mare fast. I don't want her in a sweat." He turned away, his shoulders wide against the door as he reached to open it.

I clutched the small leather pouch he had handed me. The round edges of the money inside it poked into my palms. I think I stopped breathing.

"Mr. Howard," I said bravely, "I need to talk — I need to ask you about something." The scrap of paper, with the list of things to get at the store, trembled in my grip.

Matthew Howard swung back from the door. "What is it?" he asked, without curiosity.

I took a deep breath. "It's about — It was my four-teenth birthday yesterday. It's about my wages. I wondered about how much — what wages I'll get now."

My voice sounded funny. I swallowed.

Matthew Howard gazed at me. It was always impossible to tell what he was thinking. His beard covered his mouth. His eyes gave nothing away. They were flat like a stone or the surface of a pond.

"Wages," he said, as if he was thinking about it. "Wages. Willy don't get any wages."

"He's your son," I replied. "The Barnardo people said that when I turned fourteen I'd get wages."

"Wages for a child who eats at my table and sleeps in my house," said Matthew thoughtfully.

I could feel anger rising up my throat again. Anger at the thought of all the work I did; how I grew and cooked the food that everyone ate. I pressed my lips tight to keep the anger inside.

"Forty-five dollars," Matthew said suddenly.

"Forty-five a year?"

"Yep. I'll send it quarterly to the Barnardo people."

"To the — But — but it's my money!" I cried in dismay.

"That's the arrangement," Matthew Howard said flatly. "I send 'em your wages. They keep your money in the bank for you until you're twenty-one. Then you're on your own and they'll give you the money."

I stared at him, speechless. Blood throbbed in my ears. Twenty-one before I held a cent of my own money! No one had explained this to me!

I stood there, dumb, like an idiot, while Matthew Howard swung out through the door, spoke to the dog, and went off across the yard with his heavy, flat stride and his heavy, long shadow. My knuckles were white on the leather pouch of small change. The air around me went completely still. Twenty-one! Another seven years on this farm, and nothing of my own. Nothing to help me get back across the ocean to find Thomasina. I couldn't believe it.

Numbly, I washed the dishes, swept the kitchen floor, made more porridge for Lizzy and Kathleen Howard. Then I went out to find Tom.

He was in the driving shed, backing Blossom into the shafts of the small buggy. She was an old, gentle mare with a soft black coat and a white star. When I held out my hand to her, she fumbled at my fingers with lips like velvet. Tom moved around her quietly, fastening her harness.

"Tom, how much do you get for wages?" I asked sharply.

He glanced at me. "One hundred and twenty a year," he replied.

"It's not fair!" I exclaimed. "I've just asked for mine, and Mr. Howard says I'll get forty-five a year and he'll send it away to the Barnardo people to keep until I'm twenty-one."

"It'll be a bit to get you started out in life then," Tom explained.

"I'm worth more than forty-five, Tom! You know how much work I do here!" I bit my lip hard; it was trembling.

"It's a fine pass when a child has to run a house like a woman," Tom muttered. He frowned at his long fingers, passing straps through buckles.

"Who cleaned up last night?" I asked.

"Oh, that was me," Tom said, his face turned away. *Women's work*, that's what I knew he was thinking. But he had done it anyway.

"Thank you," I said and he shook his head, like a horse shaking off flies.

"It was nothing. And you're worth more'n forty-five, Maggie, but you won't get it. You won't get it 'cause this is a poor farm, where horses are more important than crops, and where the master's heart is turned like a stone and there aren't any sons to keep things going."

"There's Willy."

"Willy ain't interested in this place. He wants to take motors apart and tinker with them. He wants to get grease on his hands and drive around in a cloud of dust like a swell."

I nodded. I knew that Willy disappeared, as often as he dared, to admire the fine motorcar that Mr. Harrison, living one concession road south of us, had bought.

"My friend from school, Mae Beth McCormick, she gets fifty cents a month allowance. Not for work she does. Just allowance to spend as she pleases. That's six dollars a year, Tom. And I'm only to get paid forty-five for all my work."

"Aw, it's not a fair world, Maggie," said Tom with a sigh. He ran a hand lovingly down Blossom's neck. "And the McCormicks' farm is over a hundred acres and has two big sons plus a hired man running it. And old man McCormick keeps things ticking over there like a clock. Now I'm away to the hay, Maggie. Be gentle with Blossom and water her in town."

"Yes, Tom," I said meekly. I watched him shamble across the yard, but I wasn't really seeing him. One hundred and twenty a year was riches next to forty-five. Did he really do that much more work than me? And *his* wages didn't go into an account in some bank in some town where he couldn't get at them. I twisted a strand of Blossom's coarse mane around my finger, tighter and tighter, until the tip of my finger went white. The mare turned her head, looked, and rubbed her nose against me. Her touch was warm and soft. I leaned against her shoulder. It's not just the money, I thought. It's because no one cares. No one cares on this farm. Something is wrong here.

After a while, I felt better. I went back to the kitchen, where Kathleen Howard was waiting. "The buggy's ready," I said. I handed her my bunches of flowers and she wrapped the ends in a wet hanky and walked out into the sunshine.

Lizzy thumped down the stairs. "We're going to town, Maggie!" she cried happily. "Can I have candy, Maggie?" Her face shone and her hair was tousled because no one had brushed it for her.

"I'll see if candy's on the list," I said, even though I knew it wasn't.

"I want those yellow ones, Maggie," she said as we crossed to the buggy. "You know those yellow ones?"

"You can show me at the store," I said. I lifted her onto the buggy seat, beside her mother, and then I climbed up and took the reins.

The buggy wheels crunched over stones and twigs as we rolled along the driveway. Lizzy squirmed on the seat between Kathleen and me. "Bye, farm," she called. "Bye-bye!" Her pudgy hands waved in the air.

I turned the mare south at the road, and she pricked her ears and pulled steadily, sun sliding to and fro on her hindquarters. I held the reins loosely. Kathleen was silent. Lizzy chattered, but mostly I ignored her, because I wanted to think. Soon she began to talk to her imaginary Lily and I just forgot to listen at all.

The sun was warm on my face and shoulders. A breeze wafted past, smelling sweetly of hay and queen anne's lace. Blossom's hoofbeats had a rhythm like music and suddenly I felt free. I had a whole day now without work, with just hoofbeats and bird song and the countryside.

I thought about how wonderful the land looked: the

rows of corn with their bright leaves waving in the breeze, the fields of spring wheat bending gracefully. Chemong Lake glittered in the sun. Cows grazed peacefully, lifting their heads to watch us pass by. Maple and elm trees cast lacy shadows across the road. The hills rolled away, rounded and soft. Drumlins, Miss Hooper had said they were called. Birds sang; robins and field sparrows. I saw the bright flash of a Baltimore oriole.

I don't want to leave this country, I thought. It's my country now.

I didn't want to leave the wide open spaces, and the way the seasons changed. I loved the flaming autumn trees, and I loved the sparkling winter days when the shadows were blue, and when we swooped down the fields on the toboggan. Days like that, even Willy and I were almost friends. I didn't want to travel far, far back along that thread that went across the sea to England. I didn't want to live beside the cruel sea that had taken my father. I didn't want to squeeze back into St. Ives, with its crowded streets, the smell of fish, the screaming gulls, the yelling children, the crowded gray cottages, the wind and rain. I didn't want to see my aunt with her cold eyes, or the minister's wife with her pitying smile. I didn't want to squeeze back into my past.

But I had to.

I had to go back and find Thomasina. I had to tell her how angry I had been all these years. I had to find out why they had loved her more, why they had sent me away. I had to find out if she missed me, if she carried me around like a pain in her bones. If she had put her memory of me in a little box, shut the lid and never talked about me. Like I never talked about her.

If I didn't get answers to these questions, I would never be happy. Even though I had wide open spaces and maple trees on drumlins, even though I had learned how to do a hundred things on the farm, like driving horses and growing flowers, unless I found Thomasina, I would never be happy. I would only be half a person, even here. Even in this country I loved and didn't want to leave. And had no money to leave. First I had to find some money, and then I had to go and find Thomasina. Or all my life I would carry her memory in my bones, like a pain, and I would have a box in my mind with the lid shut tight. And I would dream about her face at the window.

"Are we there now?" Lizzy chirped beside me. She stuck her elbows into my ribs and pushed, shaking me out of my thoughts. "Are we there now, Maggie?"

"Not yet," I said, but there was only a mile to go.

We reached the eighth concession road and turned south again. Thinly on the clear air, came the whine of saws in the lumber mill by the river. Soon rooftops and chimneys appeared among the trees. A little dog ran out from a laneway and chased after us. Wise old Blossom snorted, but she didn't shy or run away with us. Soon the dog stopped and stood panting in the road. Now we rolled past houses with front verandahs, and the lake between them was close and bright blue. The floating bridge, made of planks on logs, lay on the water's surface; someone was riding a horse across to the far shoreline. People strolled along the edge of the road. We passed the cooper's shop, and the general store. We passed the shop where Miss Findley tailored *Ladies gowns in the latest Paris fashions*, and we passed the blacksmith shop, where sparks flew and iron clanged and Blossom whickered to a chestnut gelding tied up outside. At the south end of town, I pulled the mare to a stop at the cemetery fence. The rows of tombstones were shaded by pine trees. Kathleen climbed out with her bunches of flowers.

"I'll water Blossom, and then I'll go to the store," I said. I didn't want to keep Kathleen company in the graveyard, though sometimes she made me. Today she only nodded absently as she unlatched the little iron gate in the fence. Pine tree shadows fell across her narrow shoulders.

I tied Blossom to the fence. Then Lizzy and I took the tin pail, walked back to the town pump, and carried water to Blossom. The bucket's wire handle left a red mark on my palm. Blossom blew on the water, making it ripple. Then she plunged her soft nose in and drank.

Lizzy took my hand and we walked to Dean's General Store and Post Office. Dogs scrounged around, sniffing things, barking. Lizzy wrenched her hand from mine and ran after a dog with black spots. "Come!" she shrilled. "Come, dog!"

The sudden rattle of wheels made me jump. I lunged for Lizzy and pulled her off the road, just as a fast team went by pulling a buggy. "Hold my hand!" I scolded. "You'll get hurt, Lizzy!" But I knew she was too excited to listen.

The general store was cool and dim and full of so many things that even Lizzy stood still in awe. For a little while, I just wandered up and down on the creaking dark floorboards, staring at kegs of shiny nails, muffin pans, men's bright red suspenders. Barrels of crackers, flour, sugar. There was a smell of molasses, lamp oil, harness soap. I wrinkled my nose and inhaled it all. I touched things: soft new cloth with bright colors, the smooth back of a hairbrush. For a moment I thought I had lost Lizzy, but there she was, staring at the glass jars full of candy that were lined up on the counter. There were humbugs, acid drops, caramels, jujubes.

"I want one of these," Lizzy said, putting her finger on a jar of crystallized fruit. "And one of these, Maggie, one of these yellow ones."

"Wait," I said desperately. I knew I couldn't spend Matthew Howard's money on candy. I pulled the shopping list from my pocket and looked at Matthew's writing. It was pressed heavily into the paper. I just had to buy the usual things: tea, sugar, matches, a box of Royal Crown laundry soap . . .

"Want one of these," Lizzy said. "Want one, Maggie. Want one." She was jigging on her toes, and her face was white and pinched.

"Wait," I said; I didn't know what else to say.

Behind the counter, Mrs. O'Reilly, who helped Miss Dean out, placed my packages in my basket. "Two dollars and one cent," she said. The light reflected off her glasses, so that she looked like an owl. I began to count out the change from Matthew's pouch.

"Want one!" Lizzy cried, jerking on my arm. The pouch and the money flew through the air. Coins cascaded around me, jingling, rolling across the floor. Lizzy began to cry. Mrs. O'Reilly's round glasses stared at us. With my face flaming, I knelt down and began to look for the money. When the screen door swung open, I ignored it.

"Maggie!" said Mae Beth's voice, and there were the pointy toes of her boots, almost standing on a nickel. "Oh, Maggie. What's happened?"

"Dropped my money," I mumbled and she knelt beside me and began running her fingers over the floor. My face was still red, but when I glanced at Mae Beth she giggled.

"Maybe you'll find more'n you dropped," she whispered. "I found a penny here once."

That made me feel better, and I was sure that I'd already found nearly all the money I'd lost.

"Want one!" Lizzy shrieked suddenly, so loud you could hear her out on the street. Mae Beth flinched and Lizzy's face screwed up like wrinkled paper as she began to scream angrily.

I reached out to grab her, but then came a man's boots in soft, heavy leather, well oiled, and Harold bent down and scooped up Lizzy.

"Hush," he soothed her. "What do you want?"

She was so astonished that she stopped screaming and pointed at the candy jar with the yellow pineapple acid drops.

"Three cents worth," Harold ordered Mrs. O'Reilly. "And two cents of toffees, and three cents of barley sugars."

The glass lids on the jars rattled open and shut. Lizzy watched, wide-eyed. Mae Beth and I brushed off our skirts, and I paid for my supplies. Then we followed Harold out into the sunshine. I hoped he wouldn't look at me. I hoped he hadn't even noticed me, groveling on the floor like an idiot working in a potato field. I hoped the road would open and swallow me. Or swallow that stupid Lizzy. My heart thumped.

Harold turned and gave me his slow, wide smile. "Phew," he joked. "What a fellow has to do for some peace and quiet." Then he opened the bag of acid drops and let Lizzy have one. He held the bag out to me and I took one without looking at him. I could feel the warmth of his hand through the bottom of the bag.

We walked down the street towards the lake, found a patch of grass, and sat in the sunshine. My heart slowed again. The candy was tart and sweet in my mouth. Lizzy began to pick daisies, humming to herself.

I made myself look at Harold, his thick brown hair and his wide brown eyes. They were warm looking, like horse chestnuts in October. I had known Harold for years; next to his sister Mae Beth, he had been my best friend. We had pushed each other's faces into snowbanks, and thrown wild apples at each other. But last year he had suddenly got bigger, as tall as Matthew Howard, even though he was only sixteen. And whenever he grinned at me I could feel the blood rushing through my chest, hot as a flame.

"Thanks for the candy," I said to him now.

He grinned. "What are you doing wasting a haying

day in town?" he joked.

"It's Kath — Mrs. Howard. She's at the graveyard."

Mae Beth groaned. "Mother says she's never going to get over it. Even with Willy and Lizzy, she's not going to get over the others."

"No," I said. I thought of the graveyard where my flowers were lying now. I knew what was written on the headstones in plain, square letters. The smallest stone said: *Robert Joseph Howard, born 1894, died 1897 of a fever. Suffer ye the little children, for of such is the kingdom of Heaven.* The second stone was larger, with the same plain script: *Matthew Thomas Howard, aged six years, and his brother James Frances Howard, aged eight years. Both drowned in Chemong Lake. Sorely missed.*

These were the sons who should have helped to run the Howards' farm. They were the reason that Matthew Howard had eyes as flat as stones, and that he cared only for horses. They were the reason that Kathleen sat in her rocking chair in the parlor.

"Mother says Mrs. Howard came from the city," Mae Beth said. "From Toronto. She's not really a farm person."

"Maybe she wants to go back," I said. "All she does is sit and rock in her chair."

"Really?" asked Mae Beth in surprise. "She hasn't always been like that."

"No, when I first came to the farm she was quiet, but she worked hard. She ran the house. But after a while . . . well, after Lizzy was born, she somehow . . . she did less. And this year, just this winter I guess, she's got worse. A lot worse. You know how much she kept me home from school."

"Poor woman," said Harold thoughtfully. "The Howards have always kept themselves to themselves. Suppose some families are like that. Too bad she couldn't get out more, make some friends. Must be lonely for her."

"I think she's going crazy," I said slowly. I hadn't thought that before, but when the words came out I knew they were true. "It's me that does most of the housework now."

"Did you ask about your wages?" Mae Beth asked.

I nodded glumly. "Forty-five a year, all sent away to the Barnardo people until I'm twenty-one."

"Well," said Mae Beth, "then you'll have lots of money when you're ready to start out on your own. If you get married or move to town."

I was silent.

Harold opened the bag of toffees and passed them around. Lizzy put hers in one cheek, so that she looked like a chipmunk. Harold had made a daisy chain while we talked and now he placed it on Lizzy's head. She chortled and asked for another one. Patiently, Harold's long, thick fingers began to thread more flowers.

"What is it, Maggie?" he asked without looking at me.

I didn't know what to say. How could I suddenly take the lid off that box and let Thomasina out into the Canadian sunshine, like a ghost from another lifetime?

"Forty-five's not so bad for now," Mae Beth said. "It's more than my allowance!"

"Maggie, what is it?" Harold asked again. His brown eyes gave me a long, steady look this time, and suddenly I could feel the words crowding into my mouth, ready to spill out.

"When I first came here," I said, "I told you I had no family. But I do. I have a —" My voice cracked. I swallowed. I took a breath and started again.

"I have a sister, a twin sister," I said, and then I told them all about Thomasina for the very first time. When I had finished, there was silence. Mae Beth looked like she was going to cry. Her cheeks were pink.

I glanced around. Lizzy was running across the grass. Then she crouched under some lilac trees, picking more daisies. She was talking to Lily. I didn't think she would hear me if I spoke softly. "So, what I have to do is run away," I explained.

"Run away!" Mae Beth said sharply, indignantly. "You can't just — Where would you go? Why?"

"I have to go to Toronto and get a job with better wages, where I get to keep the money. I have to save up and go back to England. I have to find Thomasina."

"You can't just do that — it's not going to be easy like that!" Mae Beth said. I knew she was scared for me.

"Maggie knows it's not easy," Harold said.

"Well then, she can't go! What would she do in a city? What kind of work? And all those strangers! She wouldn't know anyone."

"Mae Beth," I said, "what would you do if Harold was far away and you missed him all the time?"

"I'd go and find him," she said at last, reluctantly. "But

why don't you just go to the Barnardo people and ask to be sent to a place that pays better?"

"Because they will still keep the money until I'm twenty-one. I can't wait that long, Mae Beth."

"But how will you run away?"

Suddenly, an idea came to me. It leaped into my thoughts, like a fish leaping in the bottom of a boat.

"Listen, you can help. When we go to the circus in Peterborough next week, I'll run away. I'll start walking to Toronto. Maybe people will give me rides. But you can pretend not to notice I'm missing until hours later. It will give me a head start."

They were both silent, considering.

"Please," I pleaded.

Buggy wheels rattled to and fro out on the main street. The mill's saws whined. Dinghies drifted across the lake, their sails pure white. Two women wearing huge hats paddled along the shoreline in a canoe.

"Please," I said again. And then, defiantly, I added, "I'm going to run away this summer whether you help or not — so if you're my friends, you'll help."

"We'll help," Mae Beth agreed. "Bring your things in the buggy when we go to the circus. We won't tell anyone."

Harold looked troubled. "If I can get you the fare, Maggie, you could take the train to the city," he said.

I didn't know what to answer. I looked out over the lake.

Harold twisted shut the necks on the three bags of candy, and handed them to me. "Maybe this will keep

Lizzy quiet on the way home," he said. Then he stood up and pulled Mae Beth to her feet.

"Lizzy!" I called. "It's time to go!"

Together we trailed back to the main street, with all my words floating around us. I couldn't unsay them. Thomasina was a ghost here in Canada now. She went with us, past the general store, to the rail where Harold's horse was tied.

"There's one more problem," I said. "I don't know if I'll be allowed to go to the circus."

"I'll get Mother to come over and talk to Mrs. Howard. Then she'll let you go," Mae Beth said. She hugged me goodbye extra long and tight. "See you next week," she whispered.

Harold turned from the horse's head and suddenly he hugged me too, right there on the main street. He smelled like oats and horses and men's cologne. My blood whooshed through me, deafening me, setting me on fire. I grabbed Lizzy's hand tight, and walked fast back to the cemetery without looking at anything or anyone.

Blossom was asleep with her bottom lip hanging down, and Kathleen Howard was sitting by the grave-stones, staring into space.

CHAPTER
FIVE

I was hoeing corn in the garden when I heard a buggy rattling up the drive. I wondered who it could be. It was Sunday afternoon and the time of the week when people went visiting — but it was rare for anyone to visit the Howards. Like Harold had said, they kept themselves to themselves.

I squinted through the windbreak of lilac bushes, and caught a glimpse of the buggy. It was pulled by one horse: a dark bay with four white socks. Harold's horse. I walked to the edge of the lilacs and peered around them as the buggy halted by the house. It wasn't Harold holding the reins, but his older brother, Edward. And beside him was Mrs. McCormick. My heart jumped up and hovered in my throat. Then it fell deep down into my chest with a thud. Mrs. McCormick was coming to ask if I could go to the circus; I was sure of it. There was no other reason for her to come visiting on a Sunday afternoon. I hurried back to the corn and began to pull my hoe through the dirt.

The weeds were thick already: lamb's tails, dandelions,

soft young thistles that bled white milk when I chopped
them off. I threw the dead weeds into a battered bushel
basket. The corn rustled around me, brushing my arms.
It was peaceful in the garden. Usually when I worked
here I felt proud, because the rows of plants reminded
me that I had green thumbs. I liked growing flowers
best, but there was something I liked about vegetables
too — the magic way that so much came from one
small seed.

Willy and I had ploughed the garden in the spring,
after the frost left the ground. Wise, quiet Blossom had
pulled the plough for us, its shining blade biting deep
into the wet, dark earth. Willy had been told to help with
the planting too, but he was just a nuisance. He spilled
the tiny carrot seeds and spent ages picking them all
up. He planted the seeds too deep or too shallow, even
though I showed him how to measure the depth of the
earth using the joints of his fingers. He planted seeds too
close together, so that the plants grew up crowded in
crooked rows. I kept muttering at him; he just didn't
seem to be able to think about how the plants would feel.

When he started throwing bean seeds at me, pelting
them down my neck as I bent over, I yelled crossly at
him. He was wrecking the garden. He sulked after that,
and didn't work, and finally he sauntered off and left
me alone. Then I was happy; I didn't mind working in
the garden on my own. And I didn't mind Lizzy in the
garden either; she would sit in one corner and make mud
cakes and decorate them with dandelions.

Hoeing was another thing that Willy made a mess of.

He slashed carelessly through the dirt, disturbing the vegetable roots, slicing through tender pea vines and trailing pumpkin stems. Now, as I hoed alone, I kept wondering what was going on in the parlor. Would Kathleen make Mrs. McCormick a pot of tea, and serve it in the best china cups with a cookie balanced on the rim of the saucer? Or would she just stare away through the window, and keep on rocking her chair while Mae Beth's mother talked about the circus? Would she agree to let me go? When I really thought about running away, I felt hot all over, then cold. I almost hoped Kathleen would tell Mrs. McCormick that, no, I couldn't go.

I hoed and hoed. Shadows changed position. My back ached. The hoe grated on stones, and roots snapped. A goldfinch sang in the lilacs. What was going on in there? I straightened up and stared towards the house.

There was the faint sound of voices, then of footsteps. Plump Mrs. McCormick bustled around the lilacs and stopped by the garden fence. When she smiled, her cheeks shone and rounded up like plums. "Hello, Maggie," she said in her warm voice.

"Hi," I replied carefully.

"Mae Beth is all excited about the circus," she said. "I hear you'd like to go too."

I nodded and gulped.

"Mrs. Howard says you may go, Maggie. You'll need to be ready on Saturday, at ten in the morning."

"Yes. Thank you," I said. I smiled as hard as I could, although my face felt tight.

Mrs. McCormick nodded her head happily at me. Her

hat was decorated with blue ribbons and flowers, and under its sweeping brim, her blonde hair made soft puffs. "You mustn't stop visiting us now that you're too old for school, Maggie," she said kindly.

"No," I agreed, but I knew this was a lie. If I ran away, I might never see any of the McCormicks again. Not Mae Beth with her flouncing skirts, nor her mother's blue eyes. Not Harold. I was leaving them for a memory, a ghost; it was a hard choice.

"Saturday then! I'll send a lunch, Maggie — no need to worry about food." Mrs. McCormick fluttered her hand goodbye, and then she was gone around the lilacs and back to where Edward and the horse waited.

I leaned on my hoe and watched the buggy leave the farm, and then I began hoeing again. Blisters were rising on the palms of my hands. When the old bushel basket was full of weeds, I carried it to the pasture fence and dumped the weeds over for the cows to eat.

I stood the hoe in the tool shed, amongst the axes and rakes and shovels. The shed always smelled of oil, and cobwebs fluttered in every corner. Then I went into the house to churn butter.

❖ ❖

On Monday, Tom hitched a horse to the scuffler and went to hoe the turnip field. The cows would eat the turnips, mixed with chopped straw, in the barn all next winter. Willy had been sent to mend fences. Monday was wash day on the farm — the longest day of the week. I lugged water from the pump on my own, because Tom and Willy were busy. I lugged piles of grubby clothes. The skin on my hands wrinkled, and my blisters went soft and peeled off. Lizzy kept messing up the piles I had made with the clothes, muddling Willy's dirty overalls in with Kathleen Howard's petticoats. The metal washing tub was like a barrel on legs, and had a handle to rock it with, one hundred times in each direction for each load of clothes. I rocked it until my arms ached, moving the water and the heavy clothes around in the tub. Bubbles of laundry soap popped. Run away, I thought, in time with the water's sloshing sound. Run *slosh* away *slosh*, run *slosh* away *slosh*. I felt terrified.

When the clothes were clean, I fed them through the wringer, turning its stiff wheel and watching the water pour out as the rollers squashed the laundry flat. Then I piled the clothes into a bushel basket and heaved it to my hip.

The clothesline was around one side of the house, next to the orchard. It was fastened to the brick wall with a hook, and ran from there to the trunk of an old maple tree. I fastened the clothes onto the line with wooden pegs. Water dripped down my skirt, turning it limp and dark. But it was such a hot day that I didn't mind.

Lizzy had followed me out, clutching the two clothespin dolls her mother had made for her once. Their faces and their dresses were faded, but Lizzy still liked to sit in the grass and play with them while I pinned out the washing. When the line was full and sagging with the weight of wet towels and sheets and work pants, I got the long forked stick and propped the line up over my head. The sheets lifted gently in the breeze, throwing billowing shadows over Lizzy's fair hair.

I stood by the empty bushel basket and stared down the hill. In the orchard, the apples and pears were small and hard and green. In the valley, the lake was bright blue and the fishermen's rowing boats seemed as small as water beetles. The last hay smelled sweet. I tried to imagine what was over on the other side of the distant blue hills, and what Toronto looked like, and how I would get there. I would need a map, I thought. But there were no maps at the farm. Ninety miles felt like a long, long way to go. Would I get to the city safely? Maybe I was trying for the impossible.

I picked the basket up slowly by one handle. "I'm going in now," I told Lizzy, but she was in the middle of a tea party game and she ignored me. I trudged towards the house. At times I thought I should just go and enjoy the circus and then come back to the farm again. It was the only home I had, even if it wasn't much of one.

But that night I dreamed of Thomasina, crying in the rain. And the next day, while I heated the sad irons on the stove, and smoothed them over the crinkled petticoats, I thought of how I could get a map. First I had to tell Kathleen Howard a lie.

"It's about Lizzy," I explained to her that afternoon, while the irons heated again. "If I could visit Miss Hooper and borrow a reader, I could start teaching Lizzy her letters. I know she's young, but she's bright." I stopped because I knew I sounded anxious. But it didn't matter. Kathleen Howard didn't even look at me. She just nodded her head in a tired way.

"Yes," she agreed. "Yes, fine." Her words came out like little sighs.

"Tomorrow?" I asked, and she nodded once more. I tried to walk away from the parlor slowly and keep my footsteps quiet. My fists were clenched with excitement and fear. It's true, I had to keep telling myself. My plan is working. It's true. I'm leaving here and running away.

The next day, I waited until all the men were out working in the fields after lunch. Then Lizzy and I set out to walk to the house of Miss Hooper, my old teacher. I didn't think that Kathleen had told anyone about my idea of teaching Lizzy her letters. Maybe she had already forgotten about it herself.

It was a mile and a half to the house where Miss Hooper lived, and it seemed to take a long time to get there. Lizzy dragged her feet in the dust. "I'm tired, Maggie," she whined. "I want to go home. My legs hurt."

"Want a piggyback?"

"Yes."

She looked pale, and her nose was running. I held a hanky to her nose and she blew, then I hoisted her onto my back. She didn't seem too heavy at first, but she quickly got heavier and heavier. I set my mouth in a line and trudged along, not thinking about anything much, just trying to get to Miss Hooper's. Butterflies fluttered across the road. Cows mooed.

"I'm hot," said Lizzy fretfully, but I didn't answer her. I was hot too, but there was nothing I could do about it.

At last, when I thought my back would break, we came

to Miss Hooper's small, square house, separated from the road by a split rail cedar fence. Orange day lilies were flowering thickly against the white frame walls of the house; sweet peas climbed up strings. And there was Miss Hooper, looking cool and happy in a hammock beneath the trees.

She was reading a book, but when I opened the gate she glanced up. "Why, Maggie!" she cried happily, and swung her slender feet over the hammock's edge in one swift motion. She rushed across to me, in that quick way she had, with her pale green dress swishing around her legs and the sun bright in her wavy brown hair. "Maggie, have you come to visit me? And who is this young lady?"

She bent down and patted Lizzy's cheek but Lizzy went all shy and leaned against my legs, pulling my skirt over her face.

"It's Lizzy," I said. "Willy's sister. I know she's young but I thought — I wondered . . ."

I stared into Miss Hooper's wide smile and my voice wavered. It was hard telling her a lie. She had always helped me out. I swallowed and tried again.

"Lizzy doesn't get much attention at home," I explained. "So I thought, maybe — if you could lend us a reader — I hoped maybe I could start to teach her her letters."

"What a lovely idea, Maggie. Yes, there is an old reader you may borrow. Will you come in?"

I tried to pull my skirt away from Lizzy's clutching fingers, but she wouldn't let go, so I had to drag her behind me as I followed Miss Hooper up the wooden front steps into her house.

"Just wait here," she told me, gesturing to the room next to the front door, and then she pattered away down the hall. I had never been here before and I stared around. I wondered if this room was the parlor. It wasn't dim and grand like the parlor at the farm. White muslin curtains swayed at the windows, and there was a picture on one wall of ladies with parasols walking along a beach. Sun gleamed on a small piano, and above it a carved shelf held eight books. Eight! I wondered if Miss Hooper was rich. I couldn't see a map anywhere.

"Here you are, Maggie," Miss Hooper said, coming back into the room. "This is the reader you may borrow."

I gripped its worn cover tightly as I took it.

"And how about some lemonade?" Miss Hooper asked.

"Want some lemonade," said Lizzy, but when Miss Hooper laughed she hid behind my skirt again.

Miss Hooper rustled away and returned with a tray, three glasses, and a tall pitcher with frosted sides.

We sat in the yard on white wooden lawn chairs. Everything felt strange. I wasn't used to seeing Miss Hooper in swishing green dresses, or to drinking lemonade with her. She seemed younger when she was at home. I wondered how she liked living all alone in her own house, and if she had any brothers or sisters. For a moment I even wished I could tell her about Thomasina, but I knew that would be a mistake. She might forbid me to go looking for her, or she might tell the Howards that I was going to run away.

"You must keep up with your own reading, Maggie."
Miss Hooper smiled. "Maybe there is a book you would
like to borrow for yourself?"

"Oh yes!" I blurted out, flushed with nerves. "I always
liked geography — I wish I had some maps or a book
about Ontario." There — I'd said it! The real reason
why I'd come today. I gulped my lemonade and almost
choked.

"I don't have any books with maps," Miss Hooper
replied. "But maybe you'd like to borrow a book about
the first pioneers. I do have a map in the house that you
could look at before you leave, if you like."

"Yes, please," I said.

"And how is your garden this year, Maggie?"

I knew she didn't mean the vegetables. "The hollyhocks you gave me are almost as tall as me," I told her
proudly. "And the pansies have been flowering ever since
early June."

Miss Hooper smiled. "Maggie with the green
thumbs," she said. "Have you ever thought about what
you would like to do when you're older?"

I shook my head, but then I decided to tell her my
dream. "I wish I could work with flowers," I said shyly.

"I have a sister in Port Hope," Miss Hooper said, "and
she runs a flower shop. You might like that, Maggie."

I nodded, feeling the idea settle down into my mind. I
imagined myself arranging flowers in bunches, choosing
the right colors, cutting the stems to length, putting
something sweet smelling in every bunch. I imagined

how happy people would look when I handed them the flowers, how they would smile at me before leaving. How they would still be smiling when they pushed out through the shop door.

"The thing about flowers," said Miss Hooper gently, "is how much pleasure they can bring. There was a famous man once, Maggie, who said that a thing of beauty is a joy forever. If you can see beauty in things, like flowers, you'll always have joy in your life."

She gave me a big smile, and I thought that she knew how I felt — how I needed flowers to bring happiness into my life at the farm.

Then she jumped up from her chair. "Come and see the map before you go," she said.

It was in her office at the back of the house. She unrolled it and spread it flat on the table, and we held the corners down with vases. I saw Toronto, and the big lake, and Peterborough. She showed me Bridgenorth, and Port Hope where her sister had a flower shop. She gave me a book to borrow, called *Roughing It In The Bush*, and she showed me on the map where Lakefield was, where the lady who wrote the book had been a pioneer. But all the time Miss Hooper talked, I was memorizing the map, with its little threads of roads and railways leading to Toronto.

When we left, Lizzy started out walking. I kept thinking about the map, and then about the flower shop. Then I thought about St. Ives, the town I was heading back to. There was no room in St. Ives for gardens. The cobbled streets were narrow and crooked, and the front doors of the cottages opened onto the streets. There were no grassy yards around the houses. The sea wind funneled up the alleys all year, salty and cool. My mother only grew one plant, a geranium, which sat on the windowsill in a pot. Only the rich people, the upalong people on the hill, had gardens: little square gardens inside walls, with trailing rock flowers and shiny-leafed rhododendron bushes. I would never have a flower shop in St. Ives. I felt sad when I thought about this, and about how I would soon be far away. I might never see Miss Hooper again. When I finished growing up, far away in another country, I might have to carry fish through the streets, selling them at the doors like my aunt.

"My head hurts," Lizzy complained.

"You're too heavy to carry, Lizzy. You keep walking," I said, but she sat down in the dirt and began to howl. I wiped the hanky over her red face and snuffling nose; then I hoisted her onto my back. Her hands clutched at my throat.

That night I opened my trunk and thought about what I would take when I ran away. I would give my *Pilgrim's Progress* to Mae Beth, and also Miss Hooper's book, which she could return for me. I would take my three shells, wrapped inside one spare dress, and an apron. Maybe Lizzy would grow into the clothes I would leave behind in the closet. I was sad that I couldn't take the trunk. It was the only really good thing that I had ever owned.

When I went to sleep, I dreamed about Thomasina's face at the window. I dreamed about wolves howling in the corn fields, about men with dark beards staring at me with black eyes, about fast horses and buggies running me down, about long streets of gray buildings where I wandered lost and cold and alone. I woke with my heart thumping against my ribs. The house was silent. The hills were black. Soon I would be out there, alone. Soon I would be in the city, alone.

◇ ◇

Each day seemed to stretch out long, like a rubber band, but the week rushed past. On Thursday I helped in the hay fields. There was one day left before the circus. On Friday I picked raspberries and made jam. Suddenly, there were no days left — my last week at the farm was over. At bedtime, I rolled up my apron and dress, and put them in a flour bag with the shells and the books. I hid the bag in my closet, and then I blew out the candle and tried to sleep.

In the night, I heard Lizzy wailing, and the muffled voice of Kathleen Howard, then of Matthew Howard swearing irritably. There were bumps on the stairs. Lizzy's wails turned to sniffles. Finally there was silence again. I lay wide awake, on my back, and shivered even though the room was warm. Over the fields the first hint of light was sliding; soon it would be dawn. Soon Mae Beth and Harold would come to take me to Peterborough, and I would never come back.

Thomasina, I called in my mind, *Thomasina, wait for*

me! I wondered if she could hear me, in her thoughts, and if she ever called for me. I wondered what she was doing, right now, in a house in Nancledra that I had never seen.

CHAPTER
SIX

The light crept over the fields, through the oats and barley, the turnips and potatoes. Above the barn roof, the rooster weathervane gleamed like a spark on its iron stand. In the chicken run, the real rooster threw back his green head and crowed. Far off, a dog barked faintly. Downstairs, Willy rattled stove lids, and outside I could hear Tom whistling as he washed himself at the pump. In the room next to mine, Lizzy began to cry fretfully and I wondered why she had been crying in the night.

It was morning. I was running away.

My fingers shook as I dressed. I pulled on something old and worn to do my chores in. When it was time to leave for the circus, I would change into my best dress. I hurried down the stairs and measured out oats for porridge. Then I ran to the barn to fetch the milk left over from the night before. Quickly I mixed it with dried peas and scraps, and then carried the sloppy mixture to the pigs.

There were two sows in the run and when they saw me coming with their breakfast, they trotted to the wooden troughs. Their hairy, mottled bodies jostled one another greedily. They turned their flat snouts towards me and grunted, while their piglets squealed and struggled beside them. When the slop pail was empty, I went to the chicken coop and let the hens out before poking my hands into the nests. A broody hen pecked me as I slid her eggs out, but I hardly felt it. I was so excited that my body seemed to be singing as I rushed through my chores.

I carried the eggs back to the kitchen in my apron, stirred the porridge, and began to slice bread. No one else knew that Mae Beth's mother was providing lunch. If I took another lunch for myself, I could save it to eat later, on the road to Toronto. I could carry it in my flour sack.

Willy came in while I was buttering my sandwich bread. "What are you doing?" he asked.

"It's my lunch, for at the circus."

"Circus? You're going to the circus?" he asked, incredulous. His narrow eyes stretched into slits.

"Your mother said I could go."

"That's not fair. I want to go too. How come you get to go? You think —"

"I'm going with Mae Beth and Harold," I interrupted impatiently.

Willy came up close and leaned against the edge of the table. "Smelly sow," he said, very quietly so no one else would hear.

I flinched away from him. "Go eat your breakfast and —"

"Maggie, Maggie!" Kathleen's voice called.

I pushed past Willy and climbed halfway up the stairs. "Yes!" I called in reply.

Kathleen appeared on the landing in her dressing gown, her thin sandy hair hanging on her shoulders. Her face was a pale oval. "Oh, Maggie. Lizzy's sick. Can you come and look after her?"

I climbed the rest of the stairs. Lizzy was standing in the door of her room, wailing. When I knelt beside her, she burned against my arms and her forehead lolled heavily against my chest. "Ears hurt, ears hurt," she cried, putting her hands over them, rubbing until her skin glowed pink.

"Hush," I said softly, hugging her.

"She's got a fever," Kathleen murmured vaguely. "She woke me up in the night. I'm so tired, Maggie. You'd better take her downstairs and give her some medicine."

"Yes," I agreed as Kathleen trailed away. "But I have to go at ten."

Kathleen paused and turned back towards me. "Go where?" she asked.

My heart sank deep down in me, like a fishing line weight. "I'm going to the circus," I reminded her.

"Oh, not today. I don't think today will work. You'll have to look after Lizzy." She began to walk away again.

Beside me, Lizzy snuffled fretfully and rubbed at her ears. Her flushed cheeks were smeared with mucus and tears. I felt desperate. It wasn't fair, nothing was fair. I hated things, how they never worked out, how I never got what I wanted in my life. "But you said I could go today!" I shouted suddenly, words bursting out of me. "Mrs. McCormick came and arranged it! They're collecting me at ten."

My heart pounded in my ears and I squeezed Lizzy so tight that she howled.

"What the tarnation's going on up there?" hollered a voice. I glanced down the stairs and there was Matthew Howard, his eyes glaring over his dark, bristling beard. Behind him, Willy stared upwards too, his eyes glinting. "Lizzy, hold your tongue!" Matthew roared, and he climbed to the top step, his boots clumping.

"Maggie, what's the matter with you?" he asked.

I stood up. "Mrs. Howard said I could go to the circus today and now she says I can't go and —"

"Circus? What circus?"

"The circus in Peterborough," said Kathleen with a sigh. "Maggie can't go anywhere today because Lizzy is sick. I've told Maggie she must stay and look after her."

"But you said I could go!" I shouted. "You said —"

"Hold your tongue!" roared Matthew for the second time. He leaned over me; his dark face blocked out the morning light slanting through the window. "Now listen to me. If Lizzy's sick, then you look after her. Circus! You expect to go runnin' off amusin' yourself? You work here! You dose that child and then git to work! I don't wanna hear any more about it!"

He never even looked at his wife before he turned away. "Jeepers cripes," he swore as he began to thump down the stairs. At the bottom, Willy flashed me a mean, thin smile that wasn't a smile. On the landing, Kathleen

Howard drifted away again, a slim, pale woman passing silently through the morning sun in her bare feet. She went into her room, and the door creaked shut. I was alone on the landing, with Lizzy burning against me, and tears pouring hot as bath water down my face. I was so angry that all the words I hadn't said were boiling in me, bubbling and churning in my blood. I was so angry that I couldn't move.

Then Lizzy began to cry again.

"Get that child down here!" roared Matthew Howard, and I went down the stairs slowly, with my legs stiff and my muscles bunched, and Lizzy's hand burning inside mine. In the kitchen, Tom and Willy bent over their porridge. Matthew Howard opened a little cupboard above the sink and took out a bottle. He poured a tea-spoonful of medicine and pointed it at Lizzy's face. When she opened her mouth to cry, he slipped the spoon in. Lizzy gagged and spluttered, then swallowed.

"You can give her this again later. Take a look at the bottle," Matthew said. He held it out to me. *Humphrey's Homeopathic Specifics. For Coughs, Colds and Bronchitis*, I read on the label. I nodded.

Then I carried Lizzy outside. I was too angry to talk to her, or to show her the morning glory flowers opening like a curtain across the verandah, or to tickle her toes with marigold petals. I stomped across the field behind the barn. The hay stubble pricked my bare feet. In silence I sat on a rock and held Lizzy on my lap. All the time that I sat there, the sun rose higher and the air grew hot. The lake began to shine. At Mae Beth's house, people were laughing and packing their lunches to eat at the circus. Harold would be grooming his horse, smelling like oats and cologne . . .

Lizzy's head drooped on my shoulder. By the time I came back to the house, she was asleep. I tried to set her down in a chair on the verandah, but she whimpered and her eyelashes fluttered, so I carried her through the empty kitchen and up the stairs.

Kathleen's door was still shut. Gently, I put Lizzy down on her pink and brown and blue Log Cabin quilt, and when she began to whimper, I sat beside her and leaned my leg against her arm. She fell back into sleep. Her breathing was shallow and light, and her nose made a snoring sound. Some other day, remembering her, I might feel sorry for her. But today, I hated her. She had wrecked my plan. All that hoping, all that fear wasted. The walk to Miss Hooper's, the visit from Mrs. McCormick — it was all wasted. All my dreams, all my nights tossing and turning had done no good. I was stuck here. It was Lizzy's fault.

After a while, I heard the buggy come. There was a knock on the kitchen door, and Lizzy twitched in her sleep. My face was blotched with crying. I wouldn't go down and let Mae Beth and Harold stare at me in surprise and sympathy. Presently I heard Tom's voice, then there was silence. Then the buggy left. There was silence again.

I cried harder. I thought about the elephants, swaying into Peterborough at the head of the circus parade, and of the Arab horses, and the clowns in costume, and the lions in their cages. I thought about all the people eating popcorn and laughing in the streets.

I thought about Thomasina.

◇ ◇

Lizzy was sick for a week. For seven days I lugged her around, sat on her bed and kept her company, told her all the old stories I remembered from Cornwall. I felt like Thomasina was leaning against my shoulder, listening too, the way we used to listen to stories when we were five years old and our father was home from sea. At night I got up when Lizzy cried. I shushed her and rocked her and sang her to sleep. I dosed her with *Humphrey's Homeopathic Specifics*. I cooked custard, and egg pudding, and made bread and milk with maple syrup, trying to get Lizzy to eat.

And all week I was angry. I didn't see Mae Beth or Harold. I didn't talk to Tom. When Willy looked at me, I slit my own eyes narrow and mean and glared at him. I didn't speak to Kathleen, with her pale face and her silent step, who only came out of her room once in a while. She's afraid that Lizzy will die, like the other baby, I thought. I should have felt sorry for her, but I didn't. The only person I was sorry for was myself.

Finally, Lizzy's fever broke and she was cool again. She stopped complaining about her ears. I got out the reader that Miss Hooper had lent me, and began teaching Lizzy some of the letters. This way, I didn't feel so bad about my lie. One afternoon, after we'd looked at M and N, Lizzy fell asleep. Standing beside her bed, I realized that she was going to be fine. I could hear her breathing deeply and evenly in the house's silence.

I could go now, I thought suddenly. No one will notice.

The thought rushed through me, like a wind. My mind spun giddily. I didn't stop to consider. On tiptoe, I went to my room and pulled the flour bag out of my closet. The book for Mae Beth swung in the bottom of it, and I took it out and left it inside my trunk. I felt bad that I couldn't say goodbye to Mae Beth, and leave her with something of mine, but there didn't seem to be anything I could do about this now. The stairs creaked under me, and I caught my breath and held it until I reached the bottom. In the pantry, I stuffed some stale cake into the bag, with a handful of green peas and a piece of cheese. I was moving too fast to think straight. My head hummed with tiredness; I had been up every night with Lizzy.

Feverishly, like a dreamer, I walked down the verandah steps. There was no one in sight. I dashed across the field and jumped over the fence onto the road. I hurried along, my ears straining for the sounds of hoofbeats or buggy wheels, or even footsteps overtaking me. I began to run. Panic tightened my throat. Sweat broke out on my back and behind my knees. My heart jumped and banged, like the flour sack swinging against my thighs. When I was out of breath, I slowed to a fast walk. I expected to be caught at any moment.

South of the farm there was an old railway line that I knew went to Peterborough. When I reached it, I left the road and began to follow the tracks. The ties and the rails had already been removed, and the railway bed angled off southwards through the countryside, flat and level and clear of bushes. No one would see me here as I rushed away from the farm. The rail bed would take me all the way to town, and when I reached the outskirts, I would find somewhere, like a barn, to stay overnight in. Tomorrow morning, I could head for Toronto. I didn't know how many days it would take me to reach the city.

A bird flew up from the bushes, startling me. I kept feeling as though there was someone following me, but no matter how quickly I glanced over my shoulder, there was no one in sight. The rail bed stretched away empty in both directions. I began to run again, trying to find a rhythm. My old cotton dress flapped limply against my legs. I hadn't even stayed to put on my best dress, and I couldn't have run very well in it anyway. Sometimes rocks poked through the thin soles of my tight, worn boots. I slowed to a walk again. This is what I'll do, I thought. I'll walk and run, walk and run, until I get to the edge of the city.

My throat was so dry I could hardly swallow. I wished I had brought water in some kind of container. I had been stupid, rushing away without thinking things through. But at least I was free, alone in the countryside. I walked as fast as I could, even though little spots jumped before my eyes.

"Going somewhere?" Willy asked.

I was so startled, that I almost screamed, but I bit the sound off. He was lying at the edge of the railway bed, in the shade of a bush, and he propped himself up on one elbow to look at me. His long, skinny legs stuck out into a patch of daisies.

"I'm going for a walk," I said sharply. "What are you doing? Skiving off work again?"

Willy unfolded his lanky body without replying. He snatched the flour sack from my hand and turned it upside down, shaking it. The cheese and the cake, my dress and my apron, the seashells and the peas all spilled out onto the thin grass and gravel. Willy stared at them. Then he gave me a narrow-eyed look. I could see him thinking. "You were running away, weren't you?" he asked slowly.

"No."

"Yes, you were. Weren't you?"

I glared at him, thinning my lips.

He moved so fast, I didn't duck in time. He grabbed the front of my dress, bunching the fabric in his fist and twisting it up under my chin. His breath smelled like liquor. "Do you know what happens to Home children who run away?" he breathed at me.

I shook my head; his knuckles were digging at my throat. Fabric cut into my armpits.

"Last winter," he said, "two Home boys ran away on the eleventh line. They found them two days later, frozen solid. They carried them off like pieces of stove wood. And the year before that, a Home boy ran away along the train lines in Peterborough, and the train squashed him flat. Nothing left but blood and ground-up bones."

Willy licked his thin lips and leaned closer into me. I could hear him breathing. He shoved his face right up to mine. "But when girls run away . . . worse things happen to them," he hissed. "Much worse." His voice sank to a whisper.

Chills went down my spine. I yanked hard away from him, and he let go so suddenly that I staggered backwards and almost fell. I knew then that he had just been trying to scare me.

He sneered at my expression, and laughed. "Pick up your stuff," he said. "Pick up the peas and all the other stuff you stole from my father. Then we'll go home and tell him what's been happening today."

I scooped everything into my bag. I was trying so hard not to cry that I could hardly see. In silence, I began to walk back. Willy sauntered beside me, whistling. I thought that if he touched me again, I would punch him. I wondered if he would really tell his father what had happened, and I thought that he would. Willy had always been a tattletale.

Once, when I first came to the farm, I had been homesick for the sea and I had snuck away in the evening and walked down to the lake. I had waded along the soft, muddy shoreline while the sunset faded in the ripples, and a strange brown animal with a flat tail had come down through the trees and gone for a swim. It was so different from Cornwall. There was no smell of salt, just of weeds and mud and rotting things. There were no seashells. When I traipsed back through the fields to the farmhouse, it was already dark. I stopped in the top field and wiped the mud from my legs with leaves, then I went inside. Matthew Howard was at the kitchen table, reading the *Farmer's Advocate* newspaper.

"Where have you been?" he asked me. And Willy came in the door behind me and said, "She's been down to the lake." He had spied on me.

Then Matthew Howard stood up and pulled his belt slowly through his belt loops, and hit me with it while Willy smiled. It was the only time Matthew ever hit me. "Don't you go near that lake again," he said sternly afterwards. It wasn't until later that I found out about the two drowned sons.

Would Matthew Howard hit me this time, for running away along the railway line? My legs dragged, my feet scuffed miserably in the gravel. With a sinking heart, I came up the driveway. Willy had his oily fingers stuck through his braces, and he was still whistling off-key. If I had liked him better, I could have taught him to carry a tune.

Together we came around the corner of the house, and there were Matthew Howard and Tom, standing in the middle of the yard, talking about something.

"Where have you been?" Matthew demanded in his heavy, flat voice, just like he said it after I went to the lake.

"She was —" Willy began, but I was quicker than him, and I spoke louder.

"Willy's been down at Harrison's, looking at the car and drinking moonshine," I said, and I stuck my chin out defiantly at Matthew. He took three big steps towards his son, who stood rooted to the spot.

When his father reached him, Willy tried again. "Don't look at me, look at her. She —" he began, but his father silenced him with a roar.

"Is it true? Have you been down there?"

Willy stared straight ahead, with his mouth shut. Right then, I almost felt sorry for him.

"Is it true?" his father roared again, and then suddenly he cuffed Willy across the side of the head.

A red mark sprang out on Willy's thin cheekbone and he began yelling. "Yes, it's true!" he shouted. "Who cares about your dang cows and your dang stupid horses? You're behind the times! Motors are going to take over — you'll see. You'll see when you're still here moldering away on your farm. Harrison knows better. Harrison —"

"Enough!" shouted Matthew. "You smell like a pool hall. Get down to the barn and start muckin' out. Now! Move!"

And Willy went, his shoulders slumped forward over his chest. As the men stared after him, I went quietly into the house. It had been a guess, what I said about Willy going to Harrison's place. But I knew that Willy liked Harrison's car, and I had smelled the oil on his fingers when he grabbed my dress and twisted it under my chin. And everyone said that the reason Harrison could afford a car was because he sold moonshine liquor brewed somewhere secret on his farm. But I didn't feel proud of my lucky guess, or of tattling on Willy; I felt no better than him. This place is turning me into a person as bad as Willy, I thought. It would be easy to be nice if I had a mother like Mae Beth's mother, who was kind and liked to hear me sing.

I had the uneasy feeling that Willy would find some

way to get even with me. He always did.

The house was very quiet. All I could hear was my heart beating. I went upstairs, but Lizzy's room was empty. Finally I found Kathleen Howard sitting in the parlor with an old photo album open on her lap.

"Where's Lizzy?" I asked.

"She went to play at the Trumbles'," Kathleen replied. "The children came through picking berries. She went back with them."

I nodded. The Trumbles lived just to the north. They were a noisy, disorderly family. Mr. Trumble worked in the logging camps, and Mrs. Trumble moved her fat body ponderously around her shabby log house. Everything about the Trumbles was makeshift and rough: the seven children ran wildly across other farms, laughing and shrieking, falling and crying. They wore ragged clothes, coon skin hats, homemade moccasins. They were always hungry. They stole apples and pears. One morning, going out to bring the cows in, I found a Trumble boy sitting in the grass beside a cow and milking it himself — squirting the milk into his mouth. At school, the Trumble children threw spitballs, and never knew the answers. Mostly, they stayed home where their mother sang to them and swatted at them with equal lack of concern.

"I didn't know Lizzy was allowed to play at Trumbles'," I said, but Kathleen didn't reply, she just stared away.

After a moment, I went back into the kitchen and pulled the butter churn out from its corner. In the pantry, yesterday's cream was sitting in a galvanized bucket with a cheesecloth over it to keep the flies out. I poured the cream into the churn, closed the lid, and began to rock the churn's fat, wooden belly. The cream sloshed around inside it with a gurgling sound.

It was as if I had never been away, had never run along the railway line. Here I was, back in the kitchen, making butter like I'd done five hundred times before. I hummed to myself as I churned, waiting for the moment when the milk would thicken and the butter would rise greasy and beaded to the surface. If I kept humming, I couldn't think about Willy and what he had said about children who ran away. And I couldn't think about Thomasina, waiting for me at some old lady's house at the end of a long, long thread across the ocean.

So I kept humming and staring around the kitchen. This house is getting worse, I thought. The stove needed blacking, and the pine floor was covered with dust and grit and crumbs. The lamp glass was smoky and dark. On the table, the oilcloth was so old that there were holes in it, and its pattern of grapevines was worn pale and faint. The candles were almost all gone, and the butter would go sour if it wasn't taken to town and sold soon. The eggs were piled in a basket in the pantry, waiting for someone to make icing glass to store them in for next winter. In the hall, the rug needed to be taken out and beaten. Everywhere I looked, there was work waiting to be done. But Kathleen ignored it all, and I couldn't keep up with it. Things would go on getting worse.

Suddenly, I heard hoofbeats coming fast up the drive-way. One horse, galloping. I ran out to see who it could be. The oldest Trumble boy was leaning low over the horse's neck. The horse's legs drove forwards hard and fast as the boy beat it with a stick on its glistening flanks.

"Fire!" he yelled hoarsely. "Fire. Ma's house is on fire!" His voice cracked with panic as he passed me.

The horse came to a sliding stop near the barn, with gravel spurting from under its hooves. Willy came rushing out as the Trumble boy yanked the horse around, its eyes rolling and its mouth open.

"Grab some buckets!" he yelled and Willy disappeared back into the doorway's shadow.

Lizzy, I thought.

Then I began to run across the fields, with my fists clenched at my sides and my feet pounding over the grass. Ahead of me, smoke rose in a swaying column of soft gray. It billowed and quivered in the blue sky. A woody fragrance drifted to me on the breeze. I pulled it deep into my aching lungs.

I tried to run faster, the grass blurring past. I was the only one, except for Kathleen, who knew where Lizzy was. And as far as I knew, Kathleen was sitting in the parlor, staring into space.

CHAPTER
SEVEN

The Trumbles' land was surrounded by a stump fence. I clambered to the top and clung there on twisted, gray roots. Broken pieces of wood clawed at my arms and my clothes as if trying to trap me. A wild black raspberry vine almost tripped me. I sprang from the fence, jumping out as far as I could, and landed clear with a thump. My knees knocked into my ribs and air whooshed out. I staggered, regained my footing, and began to run again. Behind me, I could hear Willy's feet hitting the ground by the fence. The tin pails he was carrying clanked. Soon we were running side by side over the uneven, ragged grass.

"Where's Tom and your dad?" I gasped.

"Dunno. Dad . . . rode off . . . an hour ago. Tom's . . . in the fields," he panted.

The back of the Trumbles' place was in sight now. It was a plain cabin built with squared logs that had weathered to gray. Between them, mortar made crooked white lines. The roof was of cedar shakes, and at one end a chimney of field stones stuck up, rounded and pink and brown. Now smoke poured from the chimney and from the doors and windows of the cabin.

The yard seemed to be full of people, bright shapes rushing around in the writhing smoke. I pounded into the thick, gray cloud and the disorderly children, and began yelling.

"Lizzy!" I screamed. "Lizzy! Where's Lizzy?"

I couldn't see Mrs. Trumble, but there was a tall boy working the pump handle. Water gushed from the spout in ragged streams, sloshing into a tin bucket. Other children grabbed the buckets and ran towards the cabin, throwing the water at the walls in shining arcs. My eyes stung from the smoke and I was coughing as I ran to the boy at the pump. "Where's Lizzy?" I cried, shaking him by the arm.

"Get a bucket!" he cried wildly without looking at me. His hair flopped over his face and he was panting.

I turned and ran towards the cabin, bumping into the other children as they rushed around, some with buckets, but others simply running in circles and crying and shouting. There was a roaring, crackling sound from inside the cabin, and as I approached the back of it, a window suddenly broke with a bright, shivering sound. Glass flew outwards, brilliant as water, and my arm stung. Tongues of flame flickered through the open window, amidst a fresh cloud of black smoke. I ran around to the front of the house just as Mrs. Trumble staggered out through the front door with her arms full of quilts. Her sagging face was streaked with grime and her brindled hair, sliding down from its bun, was uncoiling on her shoulders.

"Where's Lizzy?" I screamed at her. Over our heads, the shingles burst suddenly into brilliant flame and heat waves shimmered against the cedar trees, so that they looked distorted, like reflections on water.

Mrs. Trumble threw the bundle of quilts down on the ground, beside two tipped-over chairs and a cradle.

"Got to get the table," she panted. "Help me get the table."

I leaped to grab her arms but she was already moving away, surprisingly fast for such a heavy woman. Her hips brushed the doorjamb as she plunged into the cabin's dark, smoking mouth. Desperately, I followed her.

Inside, the crackling noise was louder and the fire was whooshing and roaring in the back rooms, sounding like wind under the eaves in St. Ives. I stared around wildly, blinded by smoke. "Lizzy!" I screamed. "Lizzy!" I pushed past Mrs. Trumble's bulk, as she strained at one end of a wooden table. Heat beat against my face, thrusting me backwards. I went to the hallway and screamed into the smoke but there was no answer. Bright, shimmering light leaped at the end of the hall, where I guessed the kitchen was. I stepped forwards, calling, but suddenly flames flickered at the edge of a rug and rushed towards me like glowing snakes' tongues. I jumped back into the room where Mrs. Trumble was still heaving and grunting at the table.

"Come on, girl, help me!" she shouted, and I grabbed

the other end of the table and lifted it as though it weighed nothing. Together we carried it through the door, but then I dropped my end with a thud, and doubled over coughing. My eyes streamed tears. Behind Mrs. Trumble, the room exploded into brilliance and she cast a wild look over her shoulder and began dragging the table across the grass.

When I ran around to the back of the house again, I saw that there was nothing anyone could do now. The children were silent and still, lined up and staring at the flames. Their tin pails lay tipped and empty, scattered over the ground. Only the boy at the pump kept going, bobbing up and down on the handle as water gushed out. "Get a bucket!" he yelled when he saw me, but I knew it was too late. I stood beside the children and watched the flames flicker up the logs and across the shingles. Heat shuddered over the ground towards us, stretching my skin tight and thin.

Suddenly Tom appeared, running across the yard towards us with his mouth open and his eyes wide. He took one look at the house, and then he ran to where we were standing in the drifting smoke.

"Tom, where's Lizzy?" I cried. "Tom, I can't find Lizzy."

"How many are you?" he asked urgently, and he began to walk down the line, counting the huddled children. "Where's your ma?" he asked a girl of about eight, and another girl pointed and yelled, "There she is!"

Mrs. Trumble staggered around the edge of the yard towards us, her face blackened and her clothes torn.

"There's one of you missing!" Tom said. "Where's the seventh one of you?"

The children stared around, frightened and shocked, their skinny arms clutched over their ribs. I counted them myself; it was true, there should have been seven children but there were only five, plus the boy slumped against the pump.

"It's our Sarah," piped up a boy. "Where's our Sarah?"

The children gazed around, shrugging and muttering. Behind them, the roof suddenly gave a great crack and fell inward, blackened shingles flying through the air with sparks and ashes. Flames gushed through the hole in the roof, writhing around the chimney, clawing towards the cedar trees.

Two of the children burst into tears and Mrs. Trumble covered her face with her hands and sank to the ground. Over at the edge of the yard, the horse reared up, whinnying in fear, and the oldest boy — the one who had ridden the horse to get us — grabbed the rope that tied it to a tree. Tom ran to the pump and, snatching up a pail of water, poured it over his head and his clothes. Then he ran towards the cabin, circling it and heading for the front. I ran after him, my heart lurching. Ahead of me, in the flickering darkness, Tom was calling for Lizzy and Sarah.

"Get away!" he shouted as I caught up to him. I retreated into the edge of the cedar trees and watched as Tom plunged through the front door into flickering darkness. I could smell the aromatic cedar trees sweating in the heat. Tom seemed to be gone forever. I stared at the doorway, my eyes watering, sweat running down over my cold stomach.

Lizzy, oh, Lizzy.

"Tom!" I screamed frantically, but at that moment he staggered out, coughing and choking. Blindly, he stumbled towards my voice and I caught him by the arm and pulled him away from the burning cabin. He doubled over, retching, struggling for air. His hands were burned bright red, and when he finally straightened up, I saw that his eyebrows and his wavy hair were singed and blackened. His shirt, which had been wet, was pale and dry over his chest, and scorching to my touch. He laid an arm across my shoulders.

"Nothing we can do, Maggie," he said quietly, and we watched in horror as the last of the roof caved in, releasing a fresh column of smoke and flames.

"Maybe she's in the fields," I said desperately. "Maybe they're out playing somewhere else."

"Better start looking," Tom said grimly. There were lines on his face that I'd never noticed before, deep grooves on either side of his mouth. "Get the others to help you. I've got to wet the grass down."

But I didn't bother with the others. I just pushed my way through the cedar trees, flailing blindly at low branches. Foliage whipped across my face. Panic enveloped me, rushing and cold and white as a blizzard. I gasped and cried out, stumbling through the trees and into sunshine. Then I began to run again, alongside the stump fence. Maybe Lizzy was playing tea parties with Sarah among the roots. I didn't have breath to call their names; I just ran. Only in my thoughts, I was calling for Lizzy, again and again.

At the corner of the property, I struggled over the fence and ran downhill towards the lake, staggering finally into the cool shade under the poplar trees. Wind whispered between the pale white trunks. Sobbing for air, I stopped and bent over. Faint cries came from the hill above me, and I could see a few of the other children running through the grass, searching. Tom must have sent them.

"Lizzy!" I yelled into the tepid dimness under the trees.

I wove through the poplars and the orange monkey flowers and the tall joe-pye weed. "Lizzy, Lizzy!" I shouted but there was only the sound of the wind and a cow mooing. Between the trees, now, I could glimpse the cattails rustling in the breeze at the lake's edge. Their straight, stiff stems held up fuzzy, brown heads. Surely Lizzy and Sarah wouldn't come all this way . . . would they? I strained my eyes, sweeping my gaze through the shadows. Mosquitoes stung my arms and a dead branch tripped me. I fell headlong into the moist grass, and a spotted leopard frog sprang away from under my nose, trailing its long back legs. I might have laughed, if things hadn't been so terrible.

I turned back, away from the lake, and struggled into the field. The hill rolled up to the sky, where smoke still drifted. I was too tired to run. There was a stone pile halfway up the hill, and I headed towards it, fixing my eyes on the pale, rounded rocks. If I could just get that far, then I'd stop and rest. Another few yards . . . a little further . . .

I heard their voices.

"Lizzy!" I cried, and she popped up from behind the stones, her fair hair gleaming like buttermilk in the sun, her pale pink dress hanging crookedly around her knees, its hem torn.

I walked around the stone pile and there was Sarah, sitting near Lizzy. They had the two peg dolls on a stone, and they'd made little plates from leaves and piled hawk-weed flowers on each one.

"Me 'n' Sarah is having a tea party," explained Lizzy gravely.

I sank to my knees and grabbed her. I crushed her against my body — her torn dress, her chubby knees, her hair smelling like sunshine, her round smooth cheeks as soft as the softest deer skin.

"Lemme go, Maggie. You're hurting me."

I let her go slowly, even though I didn't want to, even though I thought I could hold her forever. She sat down on a rock and stared at me seriously with her round blue eyes. "Would you like a biscuit?" she asked, and she passed me a leaf heaped with flowers. I couldn't answer past the lump in my throat, but I took a flower and pretended to munch on it. My legs, bent under me, were shaking.

"Your house is burnt down," I told Sarah. "Didn't you see the smoke?"

Both girls stared at me, wide-eyed, and then climbed to the top of the stone pile and gazed at the smoke drifting along the top of the hill. "And your mother's worried about you, Sarah. We better get going."

I took them both by the hand, one on each side of me, and we walked slowly back up the hill to the Trumbles'.

The cabin was nothing but a heap of charred wood, smoldering and smoking. Flames licked along blackened timbers. Willy and Tom and the older Trumbles were still pouring water in a ring around the cabin, to stop the trampled grass from catching fire. Every so often they would pause to stamp out sparks and snaking flames. Mrs. Trumble was struggling with her table again, jerking it across to a wagon on which the quilts, a framed picture, and the cradle were already piled. The boy who had ridden to our farm was hitching up the horse to the wagon. Its head sank dejectedly downwards and its flanks heaved.

"Give me a hand here!" Mrs. Trumble cried, and Willy and the boy heaved one end of the table onto the wagon bed as Mrs. Trumble heaved her end.

Tom caught sight of me, holding the little girls, and he ran over and swung Lizzy against his shoulder. "Thank God!" he cried. "Where have you been?" And he shook her and swung her down again before she could answer. His face was black. He stared around at the rest of the children. "Come on, get to the wagon!" he called and they hurried to obey, scuttling to their mother who lifted the smaller ones up into the quilts.

"Where'll you go, Missus?" Tom asked.

"I've got people at Selwyn. They'll have to take me in, won't they?" she asked belligerently. "The old man's away guiding in the bush. My sister's family will have to take us in."

She heaved her great weight onto the creaking wagon seat. Her oldest son took the reins, and the tired horse leaned into the traces. Slowly the wheels began to turn. Over the pile of quilts, the small children stared back at us; their eyes stretched open above their smeared cheeks. One boy was sitting on a chair, and the tin water pails were stacked at his feet. The family cow plodded docilely behind the wagon, and a thin dog foraged ahead with its tail waving like a feather.

Soon the yard was empty. Drops of water dribbled from the pump spout. The embers of the cabin hissed and creaked, and there was so much smoke in my nose that I couldn't smell anything else. I kept staring at the ruined cabin, fascinated and horrified.

"Willy, you and me better stay here and get this lot doused out," Tom said. "Maggie, you take Lizzy home."

As we walked away, I could hear the pump start up again, squeaking and gushing. Carefully, I helped Lizzy climb through the stump fence.

"Help Lily too," she commanded me, and I held out my arm to the air.

"Come on, Lily," I said kindly. Then I took Lizzy's hand again, her plump, warm, living hand that fit so trustingly into my own, and I led her home slowly through the fields, singing to her about shrimp boats.

When we reached the farm, I took Lizzy into my garden. After the gate was shut, I sank down beside the flowers. I was very tired. I could hardly remember everything that had happened that day — how I had tried to run away, how Willy had threatened me. All I could think of was Lizzy's face with its grave blue eyes when she popped up over the stone pile. I thought about how I had felt then, how I had wanted to hold her and never let her go. Lizzy was like my flowers, I thought. She was a thing of beauty. I was sorry for how angry I had been with her because she had wrecked my running away plans. I was sorry for the times I had been impatient with her, or had ignored her.

"You sleeping, Maggie? You asleep?" she whispered, and I raised my head from my knees and smiled at her.

"I'm hungry, Maggie."

"So am I, Lizzy. Soon I'll make supper. But don't you want to see the flowers? Look, the morning glories are the same color as the sky."

I lifted Lizzy up, letting her look at the flowers. Then I picked a marigold and held it under her chin to see if she liked butter. I tickled her with the soft petals and she giggled and squirmed. I showed her how the pansies had faces, and she began to give each one a name. "Pick some, Maggie?" she asked, and I nodded. I showed her how to pick the stems long, so that the flowers could stand in a jar of water. I held sweet peas under her nose for her to smell the peppery fragrance.

I would remember her face popping up at the stone pile all my life, just like I remembered Thomasina's face in the crook of my aunt's arm on the day I left St. Ives.

The sun was low in the sky and the birds were singing. The cows were wandering through the fields and I saw

Tom and Willy cross to the barn, walking slowly as though they were tired.

"Time to go in," I told Lizzy and she trotted obediently after me, clutching her pansies. While I cooked supper, she sat under the table with her jar of flowers, and played with her peg dolls.

I knew, as I scrubbed potatoes, that something had changed today; that soon I was going to have to face up to it. I pushed the thought away, saving it until bedtime. When the potatoes were baking in the oven and the salad was washed, I went to the parlor to find Kathleen. The rays of the setting sun slanted through the west window, pooling around her rocking chair. She was asleep, with her head on one side and her thin, fair hair suddenly bright. On her knee lay an open photograph album.

"Kathleen," I said softly, and her eyes flickered drowsily.

"I've had such a nice dream," she whispered, and a faint smile lifted the corners of her mouth. She stirred in the chair, and I caught the album as it slipped. Her eyes came wide open. "Maggie, it's you," she said. "Did I ever show you these pictures? Look."

I knelt beside her chair as she turned the pages, her thin fingers caressing the yellowed photographs. "This is me," she said with amusement. "And this is my sister, Alice. Clever Alice. This is when we were six. And here is Papa, with his big mustache. How proud he was of it! He used to wax the ends, Maggie. They stood out quite straight from his face. And here is Mama. So good and pretty."

I stared at the pages as Kathleen's soft voice murmured above me. They were family portraits, with people in stiff, dark clothes and unsmiling faces. Little girls with ringlets stared back at me: Kathleen and her sister Alice wearing frilly frocks with white lace and embroidered yokes.

"And here is Thomas, my brother," Kathleen murmured, pointing at a solemn boy with fair curls and huge eyes. I thought he looked like Lizzy. "He was killed in the Boer War," Kathleen said sadly. She turned the page and her voice brightened again. "Here are Alice and I going to a regatta."

I saw two young ladies in sweeping skirts, standing by a lakeshore. Trees cast shadows over them, and sailing boats filled the background. The girls were smiling, and holding frilly parasols. I could hardly recognize Kathleen — she looked gay and carefree, pretty almost. Her hair was puffed out around her face, and ringlets were arranged over her ears. Her dress fitted perfectly, nipped in tight at her slender waist. It was hard to imagine her ever looking that hopeful, that energetic.

"Was it the Chemong Lake regatta?" I asked.

"Oh no, Maggie. It was in Toronto, long before I came here. Before I married. I lived in Toronto when I was young, you know. Papa and Mama had a big house."

She sounded wistful, as if she was longing for something. Then she turned another page and I saw a picture of a bride standing in the lacy pool of her long veil, and holding a bunch of dark roses. Beside her, a tall man stared confidently into the camera from below his top hat. He carried a cane over one arm of his frock coat.

"Here are dear Alice and dear Roland," Kathleen said.

"Alice was a beautiful bride."

"What happened to her?" I asked.

"Happened?" repeated Kathleen vaguely. "Well, nothing happened. She lives in a big house in Toronto, and she and Roland have three children. Beautiful children. And a nanny to look after them. And Alice goes to balls and parties in beautiful dresses, I suppose. Roland is rich, you see. Rich." Her voice trailed off tremulously.

"Why don't you ever see them?" I asked.

Kathleen shrugged and sighed and didn't answer at first. At last she said, "Because I'm too poor to travel, Maggie. And Alice is too busy in her big house."

"Don't you write to each other?" I asked.

"Alice used to write. But how can I reply? What ever happens here that I could tell her about?"

Then she closed the photograph album, and I wished I had kept my mouth shut. The light had died in Kathleen's eyes and she looked pale and tired again. The sunlight had slid away too, across the floor and through the heavy, dark red drapes. I could hear the men's voices in the kitchen. "Supper's ready," I told Kathleen, and she rose slowly from her chair and trailed down the hall with her shoulders sagging, the way Willy's did sometimes.

After supper, I put Lizzy to bed. I tucked her in, and kissed her, and told her a story about piskies, the little men who live in Cornwall. Then I went to my room and bolted the door. Slowly I pulled the pins from my hair and let the long red braids hang down over my shoulders. Then I undid the braids, and my hair spread over me, smelling like burning cedar wood. I sat by the window and stared out across the black, silent fields and the black ridge of the barn roof. The weather cock shone in the moonlight.

It was time to figure out what had changed today.

I thought of the burning cabin; the leaping, greedy, terrifying flames. Of how I worried that Lizzy might be in there. Of how I ran around the fields, crying and searching for her, afraid she was burning. And all that time, Kathleen had been in her parlor, looking at old pictures or asleep in her chair. She didn't even know about the fire. There's something wrong with her, I thought. She is going crazy. She doesn't care about anything anymore, only things that happened a long time ago, before Lizzy was born. She doesn't look after Lizzy.

The only person who looks after Lizzy is me.

I didn't want to think this, but I knew it was true. If I had stayed home today, and not run away, Lizzy wouldn't have gone to the Trumbles'. It was while I was running away along the railway lines, that Lizzy had got into danger. If I left the farm again, something worse might happen to her. There would be no one to protect her from Willy's mean teasing, no one to tell her bed-time stories.

If I leave Lizzy, I thought, she'll be like an orphan. She'll be like Thomasina and me, when our mother died, and there was no one left to truly care about us. And it will be my fault, because I could've stayed here and looked after her.

I sat in the window a long, long time. My legs went numb. The moon shadows changed position. The stars slipped across the sky. I was trapped here, in this square brick house. Trapped with Willy's threats, Matthew's roars, Kathleen's silences — not because I couldn't run away again if I chose to, and not because I had no money, or because I was scared of being alone in the dark countryside.

I was trapped because of Lizzy; because I couldn't turn her into an orphan like me.

Stiffly I climbed into bed, and I dreamed about red flames, and red nasturtiums in my garden, and the red hair of Thomasina lifting in the windy rain. Oh, Thomasina. I might never find her, never see her again. I was trapped, like a fish in a net, being dragged through my life behind this square brick house floating on its ridge of hills.

CHAPTER
EIGHT

"How come you never talked about Thomasina before?" Mae Beth asked.

I frowned at my needle. "It's hard to explain . . ." I replied uncertainly. "It was like, I don't know . . . like one of us had died, I suppose. It was too sad to talk about. So I just said I had no family. That was easier."

"What's it like being a twin?" Mae Beth asked.

"Well, it's just . . . it's just normal to me. I mean, I don't know how it feels to *not* be a twin." I gave her a puzzled frown and twisted a strand of hair around one finger. I wasn't used to speaking my thoughts about Thomasina out loud.

Mae Beth and I were sitting in willow chairs on the Howards' verandah, with a quilt spread smooth across our knees and hanging down around us in crumpled folds. It was decorated with a fan pattern, in many shades of yellow and green, and Mae Beth had been working on it forever. She had been collecting the fabric when I first came to the farm, asking children at school if their mothers had any old scraps that she could use. Now it was all sewn together, and we were finishing it with top stitching, outlining every fan shape with neat, tight lines of white thread. At least, Mae Beth's lines were tight and neat. Mine weren't as good.

"You must really love Thomasina," Mae Beth continued.

"Yes. But I'm mad at her too."

"Mad?"

"What's so important about her that they kept her, the relatives over there? Why did they send me away, like I wasn't as good or something? She wasn't any better than me." I bit off a piece of thread with my teeth in one quick, angry motion. Mae Beth looked at me in astonishment, her blue eyes wide.

"I'm sure that's not the reason you were sent . . ." she said lamely.

After that, we sewed for some time without speaking, while the Sunday afternoon quietness shimmered around us. The morning glory vine threw splotches of shadow across the quilt, and behind us the house was dim and silent. When I first came to the farm, the Howards used to drive to church in Bridgenorth every Sunday morning, and even though they had stopped doing this, we didn't usually have to work on Sundays. Unless there was something urgent, like the crops to bring in, we just did our regular chores — milked the cows, fed the hens and pigs.

Today, Mae Beth and her mother had arrived after lunch, in their buggy. "Mother's worried about Mrs. Howard," Mae Beth had told me in a low voice.

Mrs. McCormick had knocked and gone into the house, and, after a while, she came out leading Kathleen Howard by the arm. "Just a little drive. A short one," she was saying in her firm, friendly voice. "Some fresh air will do you good, my dear. Oh, and let's bring Lizzy too."

Mae Beth and I stood and watched as Mrs. McCormick hoisted the limp Kathleen into the buggy, swung Lizzy up beside her, and then climbed in herself with her skirts swishing around her plump hips. She clucked to the horse, waved goodbye, and left us to the white heat and the silence. Matthew and Willy had gone off to a clay pigeon shoot; Tom was fishing.

"So where is Thomasina now?" Mae Beth asked persistently.

"I guess she's with my father's old aunt. Father always talked about her like she was well-to-do — you know, had money. She lived in a nice stone house."

"So Thomasina has a good home," concluded Mae Beth.

"Better than this place," I agreed enviously. "Bet she doesn't have to slave like me all the time."

"Mother says that we shouldn't expect life to be fair," said Mae Beth, piously. "She says that Mrs. Howard hasn't had what she deserved in life."

I sewed carefully around one edge of a fan. I was trying hard to use my best stitches, because I knew that this quilt was important to Mae Beth. She was putting it in her hope chest.

"I want to hear more about Thomasina. Is she just like you?"

One more hard question. How could I explain to Mae Beth that Thomasina was just another part of me? "She looks like me," I agreed. "She has the same hair and the same eyes and her freckles are the same. But she's a little bit smaller and shorter than me, and she likes indoor work better than I do. You know, stuff like sewing. At school, we had to make wool samplers and hers was better than mine. Also, she used to help Mother to darn Father's socks. She didn't get into trouble as much."

"When did you start dreaming about her?"

"It was early this spring, when the snow was melting and the ice was breaking up. Before the grass went green. In April, I think."

"I wonder why?" said Mae Beth. She unwound more thread from the spool, and inserted it through the needle's eye in one quick, practiced motion. Then she slipped the needle deftly back into the fabric. "Maybe you started dreaming about her for a reason."

"So I'd run away, and now that's not going to happen," I answered glumly.

"Why not?"

I'd forgotten that Mae Beth hadn't heard the whole story about the fire at the Trumbles' place. She'd only heard about it from her brother Edward, who'd heard about it from Tom. So I told her all about that day: how I had run away along the railway lines, how Willy had caught me, how, while I was away, Lizzy had gone over to the Trumbles'.

"So I can't leave Lizzy," I concluded. "I'm the only one who takes care of her."

I pushed the quilt off my knees; my legs were sweating underneath it and I had a restless, trapped feeling. I laid the fabric over my chair and stretched my stiff back tall, reaching with my fingertips for the white gingerbread trim nailed to the edge of the verandah roof. Then I paced up and down the verandah, while Mae Beth stopped sewing to watch me.

"You have to find someone else to take care of Lizzy," she said at last.

I stared at her in surprise. I hadn't thought of this. "Who could I get?"

Mae Beth shrugged, and I continued to pace up and down. The lake was a sheet of glittering light and clouds shaped like pieces of cauliflower hung in the blue sky. Bees buzzed drowsily in my flower garden.

"What about getting Miss Hooper?" Mae Beth asked.

"But why would the Howards agree to her looking after Lizzy? Anyway, when school goes back, she'll be busy teaching. What about your mom?"

"Why would the Howards agree to send Lizzy to my mom?"

"I don't know."

I went down the verandah steps, the worn wood hot under my bare toes. I opened the gate to my garden and touched my flowers: the fluttering sweet peas, the blue love-in-a-mist. Suddenly, I knew the answer.

"Mae Beth!" I called, my breath catching in excitement. I pulled the gate shut behind me and hurried back onto the verandah. "Mae Beth! Leave the quilt and come into the parlor."

"Are we allowed in?"

"Just come! I've got an idea." I caught her by the hand and pulled her behind me, down the hallway and across the parlor's dark, dusty carpet to the small table beside Kathleen's rocking chair. "Look at this," I said, and I picked up the photograph album. Its dull green cover was cracked and had worn corners and edges. *Happy Memories* was written across it in flowing, gold letters.

"This is Mrs. Howard's," I explained to Mae Beth. "Come and look at it."

Mae Beth glanced nervously over one shoulder, and dropped her voice to a whisper. "Are we allowed?" she asked.

I was already on my knees, with the album laid open on the floor. "It's all right," I said. "No one's home but us. Come here."

Reluctantly, Mae Beth knelt beside me, but as I flipped through the album's pages, she leaned intently forward and I knew that she was getting interested.

"Kathleen and her sister Alice," I said, pointing at the picture of two little girls in lace dresses. "And look here — Alice getting married to Roland. And guess what? They still live in Toronto, and Kathleen says they're rich. They have three children and a big house and a nanny to look after the children."

Mae Beth's eyes were wide again. "What else?" she whispered.

I turned the page, and found some pictures I hadn't seen before. Alice holding a baby wrapped in a shawl, and christening photographs of babies in long white gowns. Then one of a big brick house with many windows, and a fancy black carriage standing in front of it. Alice was climbing from the carriage.

"Is it her house?" Mae Beth whispered, but I didn't know. I studied the windows, the silver maple trees, the shining spokes on the carriage wheels.

"Maybe," I said. "Look, here's one taken at the back." This picture showed a croquet game in progress on the smooth grass behind a similar brick house. Alice was there swinging a croquet stick, and so were some other ladies I didn't know, and two small toddlers with blonde curls.

"Look, there's the nanny," Mae Beth said breathlessly. She pointed to a tall, thin woman at the edge of the photograph, who was watching the croquet game with a baby in her arms. A wicker baby carriage was parked nearby on its high wheels. "These little children are Lizzy's cousins," said Mae Beth, and I nodded.

"Listen," I said, "this is my idea. I'll write to Alice, and tell her that her sister Kathleen is sick. I'll ask her to come and take Kathleen and Lizzy back to the city. Then Lizzy will be safe with her cousins in the big house, and the nanny can look after her."

"Oh, yes! That's perfect!" said Mae Beth. I could see that she'd forgotten about being scared of coming into the parlor, and of snooping through Kathleen's album. She sat back on her heels, her face shining. Then suddenly her expression changed. "But you don't have an address," she said.

"Oh." I stared out the window, at the horizon of hills,

as if I could see right through them to the city and discover the address of that brick house with a nanny.

"Kathleen said that Alice used to write to her," I said. "So maybe there are some old letters around here somewhere. If I could find them, I could get the address . . ."

"Oh, you can't do that!" Mae Beth said in a shocked voice, but I was already standing up and gazing around the parlor. I was sure that this was the room where any old letters would be kept. It was a large room, with one door leading into it, and one window giving a view of the lake and hills. A shiny, horsehair sofa with a curving arm stood against the flocked wallpaper. I lifted the sofa's plump, velvet cushions, but there was nothing under them. Kathleen's rocker sat near the window, and I lifted the cushion on it too. The table beside the rocker was bare, now that the album lay open on the carpet. There were two large armchairs, upholstered in dark green, and one of them held a haphazard pile of newspapers. I handed them to Mae Beth.

"Look through these," I instructed.

"I don't think we should be doing this," she protested, but I ignored her and she began to sort through the piles of *The Peterborough Examiner* and *The Farmers Advocate* while I continued prowling around.

There was a fireplace in one wall that I had never seen used. It held a dusty collection of dried, faded flowers and pinecones. Two china shepherdesses faced each other from opposite ends of the mantelpiece, and between them lay a box of matches for lighting the lamp. Behind one of the armchairs, a carved shelf held two books: the Howards' huge family Bible, and a smaller book titled *Five Hundred Dollars Yearly Profit Out Of Twelve Hens*. I didn't see how anyone could take this title seriously, and I bet that five hundred dollars was more money than any of the Howards had ever seen. Except for maybe Kathleen, when she was growing up with her rich papa with the waxed whiskers.

In one corner, a triangular cabinet with leaded panes held a glass candy dish, and some crystal wine glasses that were never used. They were dull with dust. There was a narrow drawer beneath the cabinet doors that I hadn't paid attention to before. I slid it open. It appeared to be full of papers; when I picked up the top one, I saw it was covered with fine, copperplate writing. The ink had faded. "Mrs. Mary Miller's Lemon Soufflé," I read aloud.

"Maggie, I don't think you should be in there," said Mae Beth. "I think we should go outside."

I turned to look at her. "But this is important!" I protested. "Don't you want Lizzy to go somewhere safe?"

"I don't think it's safe for you to run away," Mae Beth said firmly. "And that's what you'll do once Lizzy is with Alice."

I sighed, and stared at Mae Beth's raised chin. "I have to find Thomasina," I argued. "We already agreed about that."

Then Mae Beth sighed too, and went on shuffling through the newspapers. I picked the next item out of the drawer. Behind me, the parlor seemed to swell

bigger and grow more silent, as if it was listening to me
snooping through Kathleen's stuff, as if it was going to
pounce on me and grab me by the back of the neck. I
could feel a chill tingle where my skin lay unprotected
between my collar and my hair. My ears strained, listening for buggy wheels or footsteps, but all I could hear
was my own blood roaring through my veins. I picked
up the next recipe. There were lots of them, then hints
for running a household: how to remove stains from
linen, how to mix your own polish for cleaning copper
pots, how to tell the best time for planting a garden. I
didn't bother reading that one. Everyone knew that you
planted when the moon was full.

Under the household hints lay a collection of cards,
mostly Christmas cards, but there were one or two birthday cards as well. I glanced through them quickly: holly
berries, pansies, tulips, Father Christmas, sleigh bells —
the seasons cascaded through my fumbling fingers. I was
starting to feel panic — at any minute, Kathleen and
Lizzy would be home.

"Maggie —" began Mae Beth, but just then I found it.

"Look!" I held up the envelope. Its flap was folded
over a Christmas card with a picture of skaters whirling
on a frozen pond. "Read this!"

Mae Beth came and stood beside me. Together
we looked at the skaters, then at the writing inside
the card. *To my dear sister, Kathleen, and her family at
Christmas time*, we read. *With love from Alice, Roland, and
the children*. I turned the envelope over and there, in its

left hand corner, in the same faded copperplate writing, was an address. "Number ten, Mount Pleasant Road, Toronto, Ontario," I said aloud. "This must be it."

"If they still live at the same place," Mae Beth replied.

"Yes. But I'll have to try."

"Put everything else away," Mae Beth pleaded, and I laid all the other cards back in the drawer, followed by the household hints and the recipes. My fingers were shaking. I shoved the drawer shut, and took a final glance around the room. Mae Beth had already replaced the newspapers in the same haphazard style we had found them, and everything else looked untouched.

"Let's go," I said, and we rushed towards the door and pounded up the stairs to my room, collapsing, weak with laughter and relief, on my bed.

"Oh, that was awful," Mae Beth moaned, giggling. "What if we'd been caught?"

"But we weren't. How am I going to write this letter and get it mailed?" I asked and Mae Beth sobered and became thoughtful.

"I know. Matthew Howard has paper and envelopes in his desk."

"You can't just steal them!" protested Mae Beth.

I glared at her. "No one will know. Besides, I live here. Why shouldn't I have a piece of paper and an envelope? I've worked for the Howards for years and they've never given me anything they didn't have to. Kathleen always buys the cheapest fabric for my dresses. 'Oh, this is good enough,' she says — even though the Barnardo people

have been sending them money for my clothes!" My
voice swooped indignantly upwards, and I could feel my
face growing red.

"All right, all right," said Mae Beth. "Just hurry — my
mother will be back soon."

I sped along the upstairs hallway, and then paused to
listen. The house creaked in the silence. I opened the
door to one of the unused bedrooms. It held Matthew's
heavy, dark desk with its clawed lion's feet and its brown
leather writing top, and a straight-backed wooden chair.
I slid open a drawer in the desk, but it held only a Peter
Hamilton Co. Ltd. catalogue of farm equipment. In the
drawer beside it were scattered pieces of paper: old bills
and receipts for wheat sold and horses serviced. And
then, underneath them, three sheets of plain paper. I slid
one out and shut the drawer. Where could I look for
envelopes? I scanned the desk quickly, and spotted the
crack along the bottom of the roll top.

At that moment, the sound of buggy wheels rattled
into the Sunday silence.

I flung the roll top up, and scrabbled breathlessly
through the pigeon holes. There — envelopes! I
snatched one.

"Maggie!" called Mae Beth frantically, in a hoarse
whispering shout, from the door of my room.

I yanked the roll top back down, closed the door of the
room, and rushed to my own room, where Mae Beth's
face hovered white and pinched with anxiety. "I got
them!" I said triumphantly. Opening my trunk, I slipped
the paper and the envelope in beneath the books there,

then I dropped the lid with a click and gave Mae Beth a grin.

The faint sound of voices came from below.

"Let's go down," I said, and, decorously, we descended the stairs and crossed the hallway, arriving at the door just as Mrs. McCormick led Kathleen back in. I glanced at her curiously, to see if the buggy ride had changed her, but her face was set in the same pale, tired lines, and her eyes held the same blank, disinterested look. I thought that Mae Beth's mother looked tired this time, too. Only Lizzy seemed happy, scrambling towards me, holding up a fistful of bluejay feathers like a bunch of flowers. "For you, Maggie!" she shouted, and thrust them into my hand, their fine shafts wrinkled and bent.

"Maybe Mrs. Howard would like a cup of tea now," Mrs. McCormick suggested to me. "Mae Beth, are you ready to go?"

"I'll just get my quilt," she responded.

Kathleen trailed away, heading for the parlor without saying goodbye. I had the ridiculous feeling that she would know instantly that we'd been in there, that the room would betray us, that everything I had touched would be marked by a bright hand print. I strained my ears, waiting for Kathleen's cry of alarm and annoyance. But of course, there was only the whispering sound of her dress as she sank into the rocking chair.

Mrs. McCormick shook her head grimly. "That's a woman who's at the end of her strength," she said to no one in particular; then her face brightened as Mae Beth reappeared with the quilt folded and draped over one arm.

"That's my good girl. Did you get lots of sewing done?" she asked indulgently, and kissed Mae Beth's cheek. I noticed Mae Beth's guilty flush; she made a face at me behind her mother's back as they headed out. On the top step, she suddenly turned back.

"Oh, Maggie!" she exclaimed. "I forgot to tell you — Harold is moving to town."

"What?" I asked stupidly.

"Father's apprenticed him to a cabinet maker in Peterborough. He's going tomorrow morning, about nine. He said to say goodbye to you."

"Come along, Mae Beth!" her mother called from the buggy, and Mae Beth hurried down the steps.

I leaned on the doorjamb as the buggy moved away, but I wasn't really watching it. Instead, I was seeing Harold sitting in the back row of desks at school, whittling whistles from basswood. Once, he had whittled me a little horse from a piece of cherry wood, and every spring he made boats. People at school would trade their best marbles for one of Harold's boats, and then they would race them in the creek. Everyone came home late for chores, with wet knees and sleeves, when Harold made boats. He could make other things too: balls and skittles, bowls, butter ladles, and the patterned presses for shaping and marking pats of butter. Last year, for Christmas, he had made his mother a beautiful shelf carved with hearts and doves.

I had never thought that Harold would move away.

Now that I did think about it, I realized that Edward would run the farm when he was older, because he was the firstborn son. And Harold would live in town and make fine furniture for people, and when he was grown up, he'd have a carriage — or maybe even a motorcar — and raise his hat to people whom he passed in the street. Harold would like that, I thought. He had never cared too much about the farm and its animals. He was happiest when he held a piece of wood in his hands, and he liked being with people. In town he would make new friends, meet other girls.

By the time the McCormick buggy had reached the end of the drive and turned into the road, I had lost all my excitement about writing to Alice. I went slowly inside to heat water for tea. There was a flat, empty feeling in my stomach, as if I needed to eat. But I wasn't hungry.

CHAPTER
NINE

I clutched the letter tightly in one hand and leaned against the cedar fence. A grapevine was growing over it, and its leaves tickled my arms. Little bunches of green grapes clustered amongst the foliage. The vine tendrils were as curly as the short hair around my ears and forehead. I twisted one of my own curls around my finger as I waited; it was a habit I had when I was anxious. I hoped no one would notice me standing out here, at the end of the driveway. Especially Willy. I wondered what time it was and I thought it must be at least nine o'clock. The morning sun was already high in the northeastern sky and dew was evaporating from the thick grass.

Then I heard hoofbeats and after a moment Captain appeared, stretching out his long dark legs in a swinging trot. My heart gave two bumps in my chest, and I stepped onto the road feeling lightheaded and breathless.

When he saw me, Harold pulled his horse to a walk. "Maggie!" he called, grinning, as he swung down from Captain's high back and landed beside me. His cheeks were flushed above a new shirt of crisp, blue cotton. His thick hair was combed back with water and his dark eyes shone. I didn't see how he could be so happy about going away and leaving us all behind.

"Did Mae Beth tell you?" he asked. "Father's apprenticed me and I'm going to learn how to make all kinds of things! And I'm going to live with the family. Mr. and Mrs. Jameson are great folks and they have a son the same age as me. And Father is paying for me to keep Captain there, with Mr. Jameson's horse, so I can ride home on my half-days."

"That's wonderful," I said, trying to make my voice sound glad. Then I changed the subject quickly, before Harold could notice how completely unglad I felt. "I was wondering if you could mail my letter?" I held the envelope out, with the address on Mount Pleasant Road facing upwards, and Harold took it immediately.

"Of course," he agreed.

"I don't have a stamp," I mumbled, staring at my feet.

"Maggie, it's all right. I can put a stamp on it. And I have something for you." He reached into one pocket and pulled out a crumpled envelope which he handed to me. "It's not much," he said earnestly, "but I hoped it would help. You might, you know, need it sometime. If you run away to the city. I'm sorry I couldn't get you more."

While he was talking, I stared into the envelope at the two dollar bill. No one had ever given me two dollars before, and I didn't know how to thank Harold. When I finally glanced up, I saw a worried wrinkle in his fore-head. Maybe he thought I was offended because I was so quiet.

"I will always remember this," I said solemnly, and Harold looked relieved.

"If you do leave . . . be really careful, Maggie."

"I'll manage," I said, and suddenly Harold laughed, creasing up his tanned cheeks and his brown eyes.

"I know you'll manage. You were the only girl at school with a good aim. Your snowballs and apples always hit their target. Ouch!"

I began laughing, too, as Harold swung back into the saddle and shortened the reins. Captain's ears flicked forwards. "I have to keep going, Maggie. But don't worry — I'll send your letter from town. Goodbye!"

His heels nudged Captain's bay flanks, and the two of them moved forward. All my laughter drained away. I stood in the road, with my right hand in my apron pocket and my fingertips lying against Harold's envelope with the money inside. When Harold reached the bend in the road, I called goodbye one last time, and he half-turned in the saddle and waved. For a moment, his cheerful whistling came faintly back to me, and then I was standing alone in the dust, with only the sound of birds singing in the cedar trees. I turned slowly and walked towards the farmhouse. I almost wished that Harold had given me another hug, like the one that had set me on fire outside Dean's General Store. Right now, all I had was that flat, empty feeling again.

I sighed, and wondered what piece of work I should

start on. Matthew had told me and Willy to clean out the root cellar today. This was a dirty job that I hated. The cellar always smelled of mold and mildew, and spiderwebs would wrap themselves stickily across my face. The leftover potatoes were unfailingly rubbery, with long, soft, pale shoots that made me think of drowned people's arms. The remaining apples would be withered and wrinkled, and sometimes when I picked one up, my fingers would sink through into brown, rotted pulp. Anyway, Willy had probably disappeared by now, and I would have to work in the cellar on my own. Maybe that would be easier. I wouldn't have to worry about him slinking up beside me in the dark, stroking flabby carrots against my arm and making me squeak with fright.

"Maggie!" called Lizzy's small voice, and I glanced towards the orchard. She was playing in the grass under the apple trees, and I strolled over to talk to her. I was just putting off that moment when I would have to yank up the cellar's heavy wooden door and descend the dusty steps.

"Hello, Lizzy. What are you doing?" I asked.

"Me 'n' Lily are looking for fairies," Lizzy replied.

"Fairies! Have you found any?"

"No. Maggie, you know those little men . . . those little men who come — if you put milk out at night?"

"Ummn," I grunted. I was only half-listening to Lizzy's stumbling words. I had pulled down a bough and was looking at the pink-skinned snow apples. They were early fruit, and soon they would be ready for picking and making into applesauce. I wondered how I would ever get it all canned if Kathleen stayed in the parlor, and whether Mae Beth and her little sister Minnie could come and help me. We could have a canning bee.

"Will they?" asked Lizzy.

"What?" I said. I let go of the branch, and the apples bobbed on their short stems. I wondered why the pigs were making so much noise, squealing and grunting. They'd been fed hours ago, but maybe one of them had found a choice morsel left over, and now they were all fighting for it.

"Maggie?" asked Lizzy patiently.

"I don't know," I replied, which was true — I didn't know what Lizzy was talking about. I thought I should go and check on the pigs. "Are you coming?" I asked Lizzy, and she trotted after me. We went out from the orchard's thin shade, crossed the hot grass, and rounded the corner of the house.

I began to run.

"No! No!" I shouted in anguish. "No!"

When I reached my flower garden's open gate, I was moving too fast to stop. I skidded right through and barged into the solid flank of the closest pig. It was like running into a wall. The sow swung her head around and squealed at me. I glimpsed her long teeth, but I was too upset to care. I beat her with my fists, pummeling thick skin and flaky mud and coarse, white hair. "Get out! Go! Go!" I yelled breathlessly, and the sow wheeled around to face me. Her little eyes were glittering over her drooling snout. She charged at me, but I jumped sideways and fell over a piglet. I landed on my side, amongst the trampled flowers, the broken stems, and torn petals. I leaped to my feet, beating at the piglets. They scrambled away, squealing and jumping over each other.

One piglet had a sweet pea vine wrapped around its hind feet. It bucked and kicked as it tried to get free. Another piglet dashed past me with its snout wrapped in morning glories. The two big sows went on ignoring me, rooting through the plants and the churned-up dirt.

"Maggie! Here's a stick!" shouted Lizzy, and she threw it towards me.

"Get up on the verandah!" I yelled, and I caught the stick with one hand as it cartwheeled through the air. It was dry and crooked, a branch from a maple. When I whacked the nearest sow across the back, it broke in two pieces. I changed my grip and whacked the sow again with the short piece that was left. The sow let out a sharp, explosive grunt and swung around.

This time, I was determined to get rid of her. I jumped to one side and went on hitting her and yelling. Suddenly she began to run, squealing and grunting, her fat belly flopping and her trotters making sharp marks in the yard. I ran after her, whirling my arms like a windmill. Piglets streamed past me, a tangle of speckled backs. Then I returned to the garden, and rushed at the other sow. She had her snout buried under a tangle of hollyhocks, and when she turned her head around I saw pieces of corn fall from her wet mouth.

"Get out! Get out!" I yelled. I could hardly pronounce the words; fury twisted their shape, made the wrecked garden shimmer in contorted blobs before my eyes. I stumbled towards the sow and began to whack her. She lunged at my legs and I heard my dress rip. Then she scrambled through the open gate and rushed across the yard with her tightly curled tail bobbing.

The last two piglets raced past my feet, and I was alone in my garden, gasping for air. I could feel lichen on the stick tickling my palm and I dropped it.

"All right, Maggie?" asked Lizzy's small voice. Her frightened face hung over the side of the verandah. I didn't answer her. I wasn't all right. I was so furious that I was shaking all over. My chest burned, my throat was dry and my spit was slimy. My hair was hanging over my face, and as I panted I felt a pin slide from my braids down the back of my dress. I let it fall.

My garden was wrecked. The marigolds were tattered pompons of yellow in the debris. Broken hollyhock stems stuck up like trees in a ruined forest. The vines were tangled and snarled like balls of wool. White clumps of roots lay beside holes the pigs had dug with their strong, tough snouts; the chrysanthemums would not flower later this fall. I sank to my knees and turned over petals between my fingers. They were ripped, shredded, soiled. I gulped and shook and wondered what Miss Hooper would say if she could see me now. A few stray kernels of corn still lay where they had been sprinkled amongst my flowers.

"Guess you didn't latch the gate right this morning," said Willy. He lounged just outside the fence, hands in pockets.

I was beside him so fast that I didn't feel myself going through the gate. Everything blurred around me. Willy's face floated in a red haze. I grabbed his shirt with both hands and started kicking him. His shins were hard as sticks under my bare feet, and as I shook him I could feel his ribs against my knuckles.

"You did it!" I screamed. "You opened my gate. You let the pigs out. You put the corn there!"

I was sobbing for breath, kicking and twisting as Willy lunged around, trying to get free of my grip, and kicking me back. Pain shot through my legs. My head wobbled on my neck as Willy shook me; my teeth clattered together. Willy's face approached and receded through the red haze.

Suddenly hands grabbed my neck and another sound joined the bedlam of Lizzy's shrieking, my own voice yelling, Willy shouting swear words.

"Stop it!" roared Matthew Howard, and he pulled us apart so suddenly that we both fell over backwards. Willy sprang back up, quick as a cat, but I sat where I fell.

"Willy, the pigs are out. Go and git them back," Matthew thundered. "Maggie, git up! Start cleanin' the root cellar. You should be ashamed of yourself."

"She —" began Willy.

"He let the pigs —" I tried to say.

"Shut up! You need a strappin', the pair of you!" Matthew bellowed. He loomed over me, breathing heavily until Willy went off in the direction the pigs had taken. Then he grabbed me hard by one arm and jerked me to my feet. "Git going," he said, and at that moment we heard the buggy wheels. Matthew let go of my bruised arm and strode around to the front of the house to see who was arriving.

I staggered back to my garden on shaking legs, and stared at the wreckage. Now that summer was half over, it was too late for anything to grow back. For this year, my garden was ruined — Willy had got his revenge for the time I tattled on him about cars and moonshine whiskey.

I slumped down on the verandah steps, feeling sick. Lizzy crept to my side, and laid a pudgy hand on my knee. "All the flowers are spoiled," she whispered tentatively.

"Yes."

I thought of myself flying at Willy, kicking and shaking him in a haze of rage. I burned with shame. Once, Thomasina and I had seen two fishwives fighting on the harbor wall. They had scratched with their nails, and kicked with their hard boots, and torn each other's aprons and shawls. When we told our mother about it, she had shaken her head disapprovingly and sniffed. "No better 'n animals," she'd said.

That was me. No better than that. This farm was turning me into a wild person. What would Mae Beth and Harold think if they heard what had happened? I imagined Mae Beth's wide, astonished stare, and Harold's muttered exclamation. She's just like an animal, they would both think.

"Who's that man?" Lizzy asked.

"What man?" I raised my eyes, and saw, coming across the yard, Matthew Howard with a tall man in a dark suit beside him. The man walked with a firm, measured

stride, every step just the same length, and he held his
back stiff and his head high. His nose made a beak-
shaped shadow across his chin, and his eyes were deep,
sunk under the brim of his black hat. It was Mr. Walker,
the Barnardo home visitor from Peterborough. I wished
I could disappear into the shadows under the verandah.

"Maggie, Mr. Walker has come to see you," Matthew
said flatly, without looking at me. "Take him into the
kitchen and make him a cup of tea." Then Matthew
turned to the man beside him, shook his hand, and
headed off towards the barn. Mr. Walker's long shadow,
as stiff and straight as he was, fell across the grass to
my feet.

I raised my eyes at last, and stood up. "Come in," I said.

In the kitchen, Lizzy scooted under the table and
stared at Mr. Walker, who ignored her. I took the kettle
out to the pump and filled it, wondering why he'd come
today of all days. He was supposed to visit once every six
months and check on me, but sometimes he didn't show
up at all.

While the kettle was heating on the stovetop, I sat
down opposite Mr. Walker at the kitchen table, and
stared past his shoulder. I knew that he was glaring at me
with cold eyes; that he'd noticed my falling down hair,
my torn dress, my fingernails rimmed with dirt from
hitting the pigs. Mr. Walker noticed everything.

"I hope you are being a Godly and hard-working girl,
Maggie," he said frostily, as though he very much
doubted that I was being either.

"Yes," I muttered, staring at his long beard. Its bushy,

gray strands hung all the way down his shirt front, but there was nothing messy about it, although it reached almost to his belt. Every strand seemed to know where its place was, and lay there tidily. Mr. Walker reminded me of the picture of Noah that was in the front of the Howards' family Bible. Noah had a long beard too, and stood in the door of his ark holding a big staff and gazing sternly at the animals as they arrived in pairs — as if he was only looking after them because he had to, not because he liked them.

"Mr. Howard tells me that he has arranged for suitable wages for you, Maggie. I hope you appreciate his generosity," said Mr. Walker in a measured tone.

I opened my mouth to protest; there was nothing generous about paying for my hard work. Then I shut it again. I didn't have the energy to argue, and anyway, I knew that Mr. Walker wouldn't listen. He was deaf to any opinion besides his own.

The kettle boiled and steamed, and I made tea and poured Mr. Walker some in a chipped mug. I couldn't be bothered with the china.

"The Barnardo Society has given you an excellent start in life, Maggie. Thanks to them, you have escaped your dismal past and are now firmly set on the path of a new life. You have been given a beginning in a country rich with opportunity."

I blew on my tea and let him drone on. I'd heard it all before.

"I trust that you will repay God's goodness through acting in a responsible and worthy manner. I hope to hear that you are behaving at all times as befits your station in life, and your gentle sex."

Maybe he'd heard about the fight, I thought. Or maybe he was just referring to my disheveled appearance. For a moment, I almost wished that he'd seen the fight — I could imagine how shocked he would have been! Even his beard would have shaken with disbelief. I suppressed the smile that tugged at the corners of my mouth.

"It has come to my attention that your sister has been sent to Canada under the auspices of Dr. Barnardo," said Mr. Walker, in the same regulated tone of voice.

My tea slopped onto my knees, scalding hot.

"My sister!"

"Do not stare at me with your mouth hanging open in that unmannerly fashion," Mr. Walker remonstrated, stroking his beard with stiff, straight fingers.

"My sister?"

"She arrived in April, and is currently with an excellent family."

"Thomasina? My twin sister?"

Mr. Walker expelled an exasperated whistle of air through his strong, inflexible nose. "You are conversing like a fool," he stated. "Your twin sister, Thomasina, arrived on the ship *Cornelian* in April of this year. She disembarked in Halifax and came by train to Hazelbrae House, in Peterborough. She is now with the Smith family."

"Where?" I cried wildly. Lizzy's face stared up at me intently. I set my mug onto the table, before I spilled tea on her. My fingers were stuck through the handle, and I struggled to pull them out. They were shaking again. "Mr. Walker, Sir, where is she now?"

"The Smith family have a farm on Settler's Line, near Keene. Thomasina is helping with the children."

He shot his long straight legs out, and rose to his feet. "I must be on my way," he pronounced, setting his black hat back on the center of his head in his usual deliberate, precise manner.

I scrambled to my feet, bumping into the table in my haste, slopping my tea again. "But, Mr. Walker — my sister! Thomasina! When can I see her?"

"Possibly some meeting might be arranged at a later, more convenient date. I understand that the barley harvest is soon to commence and that your presence is required here. Patience is a virtue of especial value in women, Maggie. Good day."

His back was straight as a rod, his coat smooth and tight across it. He seemed to go down the steps without bending his legs, gave my trampled garden one swift, disdainful look, and crossed the yard towards his buggy.

I gathered my skirts in both hands and ran after him. "Mr. Walker! I need to see her! I must see her!"

He gazed down his nose at me, and flicked the buggy whip. "Cultivate all the virtues esteemed in women, Maggie," he advised. "Be content with your lot in life and God will reward you as He sees fit. Your sister is happy where she is. I advise you to emulate her."

The buggy wheels began turning, and Mr. Walker sailed down the driveway, staring straight ahead above his well-disciplined beard.

I sat on the grass, dazed. Thomasina here, in Canada. In Keene. I tried to visualize Miss Hooper's map, with its threads of roads and railway lines, its dots for towns. Keene was a village south of Peterborough. I tried to imagine how many inches away it had been on the map. Maybe it was twenty miles from here. Twenty miles! That was nothing, nothing at all. It was two inches on a map. It was a piece of thread too short to sew with. It was three days' walking.

April, I thought. April, when the snow melted and the ice cracked and broke into pieces. April — the month I began to dream about Thomasina calling to me through a pane of glass, her red hair swept with wind and rain. Maybe you began to dream about her for a reason, Mae Beth had said. And it was true, I thought now. She had been getting closer to me all the time. A chill ran down my spine and I shivered as if a cloud had passed in front of the sun.

Thomasina.

Neither barley harvest nor Mr. Walker could keep me from finding her.

CHAPTER
TEN

In the evening, long after Mr. Walker had driven away, I bolted the door of my room and got ready for bed. Standing in front of the closet's mirror, I held my candle up high. The flame reflected with a soft glow. Light washed over the coarse, white cotton of my nightie and the thin oval of my face. The crack in the mirror ran right through my reflection, from the top of my red head to the nightie's crooked hem. On either side of it, my reflection had half a mouth, half a nose, one ear, one eye. Both eyes stared back at me, deep blue and brooding.

If one half of the reflection was Thomasina, I thought, would that side look any different now? Or would it be just the same? In my dreams, she always looked like a little girl, the person she had been when I left St. Ives. But I knew this would not be the way she looked now. She would be taller, perhaps the same height as me. Did she plait her long hair into two braids and pin them around her head, the way that I did? And would her hair curl around her ears and across her forehead? Would her reflection fit perfectly over mine: same length of thin

strong arm, same curve of calf, same high instep on each
bare foot?

My eyes traced the mirror's crack, top to bottom,
bottom to top. If one half of the reflection was
Thomasina, what was better about that half? In what way
was she more lovable than me? Could a reflection tell me
what the Cornish relatives had seen, when they chose to
keep her?

My arm, holding up the candle, began to ache and hot
wax dribbled down the candle's lumpy sides. I blew the
flame out, and the mirror became a dim rectangle holding the ghostly shimmer of my nightie. Who knew, in
the dark, which girl's face hung on each side of that
crack? I went to my window and stared out. Lightning
flickered and glimmered above the hills and thunder
muttered far off, like distant wagon wheels.

I tried to imagine what Thomasina had been doing
during all the years I'd spent here, walking to school,
churning butter, chasing pigs. I pictured her in the
kitchen of a big stone house, with the black range sending out a cozy warmth. She was sitting in a high-backed
chair, on a plump cushion, sewing. I always pictured my
father's aunt as old, with a frilled bonnet surrounding her
kindly, bright-eyed face. Maybe she told stories to
Thomasina while Thomasina sewed. Maybe they shared
hot toast and honey when the wind moaned under the
eaves and rain buffeted the windows. In this picture,
Thomasina was always neat and clean in hand sewn
smocks, and on the kitchen wall hung the bright wool
sampler she had made when we were both at school in

St. Ives. It was easy for the old aunt to love Thomasina, with her curled smile and her rosy cheeks, and her fine, straight stitching.

But now, this picture didn't work anymore. Thomasina was in Canada. I wondered if it was hot on Settler's Line, and whether Thomasina could hear the same thunder and watch the same spidery webs of lightning that I could. Why had she been sent away across the ocean, to work for a family called Smith? Had something happened to my father's old aunt? I couldn't make the pictures work in my head; couldn't see how Thomasina had come here, to this country of suffocating summer nights and sharp winter brilliance. Did she know how close we were, only inches apart on the map?

I hoped that she wanted to see me again.

It was too hot to sleep, and when I lay on my hard bed, darkness pressed down on me like a weight. I struggled to breathe, drawing thick air in slowly. Static electricity sparked in the darkness when I moved, and the hairs on my arms stood straight up. The night seemed alive around me. I squeezed my eyes shut, afraid to glance at the mirror in case it held a ghostly shimmer; in case Thomasina's face was there on one side of the crack.

After this, there were storms almost every night. People said it was the hottest August they could remember. The heat swelled up, bigger and bigger, pressing down on us. The lake lay flattened and docile, colored with reflections. The trees hung soft and limp. In the fields, the wheat ripened, turning the color of rust, and the whiskered barley swelled plump and milky. Tom and

Matthew walked along the edges of the barley every day, rolling the kernels between their fingers, judging how long until cutting time, scanning the horizon for rain.

Willy and I avoided each other. There was something sullen and brooding about him, I thought. He hardly ever raised his eyes from his boots, and he often disappeared for hours. I reckoned he was walking the old railway line to Harrison's, but I kept my mouth shut. Kathleen retreated further into her imaginary world and often didn't come out of the parlor, even for meals. Lizzy was listless, and complained about the heat. I didn't see Mae Beth; perhaps she was working hard at home, or perhaps she was too busy having fun to visit me. I knew that, other summers, she'd attended canoe races and sailing regattas, church socials and wagon rides. Maybe she would even go to town and see Harold. I wondered if Harold ever missed us. Me. I wondered if he missed me.

By day, I dragged myself through the hazy air like a swimmer moving slowly under the water. At night, heat lightning flickered and shuddered across the sky. I lay awake hour after hour; then, when I fell asleep, I dreamed of Thomasina.

At first, after Mr. Walker's visit, my dream was the same old dream — but then it began changing. It got so that, through the wet, green glass, I could hear Thomasina's voice. She was calling my name. "Wait for me!" she pleaded. "Maggie!" Then, for the first time, I began to move in my dream: stepping to the window and struggling with the rusted latch. I pushed and pulled on the thin, cold metal, but it was seized in position and I couldn't open it. I wept with frustration, the metal black and hard in my hands, Thomasina's face fading away into the rain like a reflection fading in a mirror when the candle is blown out. One night, I got the window open but I was too late — she was gone. I tried to call her name, but no sound came out of my mouth.

I waited and waited for word from Alice in Toronto. Had Harold remembered to mail my letter to her? Maybe he'd dropped it from Captain's back, and the wind had blown it away before he'd noticed. Or maybe he'd arrived at the Jamesons' and been put straight to work, and hadn't had time to mail it. Or maybe he didn't know where the post office was in town. And, if he had mailed it, had Alice received it at Number Ten, Mount Pleasant Road? Had she read it at some shiny mahogany table set with a silver teapot and lace doilies? Would she care enough about Kathleen to do anything? Or would she just fold the letter up again with her tapering, scented fingers, drop it onto a silver tray with other papers, ring the bell for more tea — and forget all about her sister?

I hoped that I had said the right things. Maybe something about my words would displease her, or maybe she wouldn't believe them. I had used my best penmanship. *Dear Alice*, I had written, *I am sorry that I do knot know your last name. I do knot mean to be forward. I think you should know that your sister Mrs. Kathleen Howard needs sum help. She is knot well and there is no one to take proper care of Lizzy. She is your little children's cousin. Respectfully yours, Maggie Curnow*. The lines repeated themselves in my head no matter what I was doing. *Respectfully*

yours . . . I think you should know . . . she is not well . . . over
and over, while I picked apples and fed hens and washed
snap beans for supper.

But the days dragged past, and no answer came.

I dreamed about an empty window — no face, no
red hair, only rain. I struggled with the latch fiercely,
desperately. When the window flew open, the wind
rushed into my throat. "Thomasina! Thomasina!" I
cried, but there was no answer. Waves rushed across
the bay, white capped, menacing, filled with bobbing
potatoes all growing long, pale shoots. I woke up with
my heart thudding in the dark.

The barley harvest began. Matthew harnessed three
horses to the reaper, and drove it to and fro across the
field. Its long blades cut the barley stems, then as they
fell, wooden paddles scooped them up and dropped them
onto the reaper belt. Around and around the paddles
swept, like windmill blades. Ahead of the reaper, the
barley swayed tall and shining; behind it, the neat bun-
dles fell to the ground. Willy and I bound the sheaves of
barley together with twine. Some folks had the new, self-
binding reapers, but Matthew Howard's equipment was
old and out of date. After Willy and I had bound the
sheaves together, Tom came behind and stood them up
in stooks.

My cotton blouse smelled hot, as hot as when I ran the
irons over it. Sweat prickled at the back of my neck and
my knees. The shimmering air pressed in around me. On
the second afternoon, as I walked between one sheaf of
barley and the next, I cried out and stumbled. White,

blinding pain flashed through me, darting from my ankle up through my body like flame. I fell, clutching my knobby ankle bones between my palms.

"What is it, Maggie?" Tom asked beside me. His bent knees swam before my eyes.

"Aw, she's just fooling around," Willy said morosely, and walked on to the next sheaf.

I couldn't speak. I was cold all over, as cold now as I had been hot only a minute before. Tom lifted my hands away from my ankle and rubbed his long fingers over the skin. "I don't see anything," he said in a puzzled tone.

I drew a breath and looked. There was nothing to see. "It's throb — throbbing," I stuttered. "Tom, what's wrong with it?"

He shook his head and felt around my ankle again. "Guess you sprained it, Maggie," he said. "Just go easy on it now."

I took his hand and let him pull me to my feet. The pain in my ankle settled into a dull ache. I knew I hadn't sprained it; the pain had begun *before* my fall. It was the pain that had made me stumble, its sudden, fierce flare sending me down onto the stubble. I was mystified. Shakily, I hobbled after Willy and began binding sheaves again.

All afternoon my ankle throbbed, but it didn't swell or show any bruise. I wished there was someone around I could talk to about it, someone who could explain what had happened. I wanted Mrs. McCormick's bustling cheerfulness, or Miss Hooper's quick firmness.

That night I dreamed that the window opened and I

fell through it, down and down through green light and wind and the sound of Thomasina crying my name. "Maggie, Maggie!" she called, but she was invisible.

By the time the barley was cut and stooked, the snow apples were ripe. Tom and Willy and I spent two days in the orchard, filling bushel baskets with round, red apples. We ate as many as we wanted, biting into soft flesh and juice. There was nothing as good as an apple straight from the tree. Lizzy ate until she cried with the stomachache. I got stung by a yellow jacket. Tom stood on the top step of the ladder and shook the branches; apples rattled down with soft thuds. Willy balanced stones along the top of the fence and threw his cores at them.

Then I spent days in the kitchen with Willy. We cored apples, and sliced apples, and hung the slices to dry on strings across the verandah. We chopped apples, and cooked them, and mashed them into applesauce. For days my skin and hair were scented with the thin fragrance of apples. We worked in silence, avoiding each other, being careful not to be on the same side of the room or the same side of the table.

"This place can't get to me," Willy said once, out of the blue. "I'll be gone down the road soon enough."

He folded his thin lips into a line and lapsed back into silence when I glanced at him. There were moments when I felt sorry for Willy, with his bony shoulder blades and his worn shirts missing buttons and his shabby pants with ripped knees. I remembered what Mae Beth said about life not always being fair, and I thought that maybe

Willy might have liked a different life. Maybe he would have been a different person then. I tried to imagine Willy being like Harold, with a warm smile and bright eyes.

"Whatcher staring at?" Willy asked suddenly, and I dropped my gaze to the apples again.

"Nothing," I said. I couldn't imagine him being like Harold. Maybe there was more to it than luck and fairness, I thought. Maybe people could decide for themselves how they wanted to act in life. I wondered about Thomasina, about what kind of a person she had turned into from living with an old lady at Nancledra. If she was hot tempered. What kind of things made her laugh. If she liked flowers.

When enough apples were dried, or sauced and canned, the rest were stored in the root cellar. Then Willy went out to hoe turnips. Still, no word came from Alice in Toronto.

One night, I dreamed that Thomasina came right to the window and pressed her face against it. The glass cracked. A thin, crooked line split her face into two. Each side had an eye, an ear, half a nose, half a mouth. I woke with my mouth dry, and the heat torn apart with thunder. Drops began to fall in a soft rush. Wind swooped through the orchard and rattled the windows. Rain hammered against the glass and roared over the roof. The maple trees creaked and groaned. I sat up in bed, hunching my knees to my chest, and wrapping my arms around them. I was in my dream, terrified, alone in the rushing rain. Alone, alone.

The handle on my door rattled. The skin crawled on

my neck. Then small fists thudded against wood and I was back in the real world.

"Maggie!" Lizzy wailed. I got up and slid the bolt across. Lizzy pattered to my bed and climbed in, whimpering with fear.

"Hush, it's all right," I said as I climbed in beside her. She curled against me, warm as a puppy, her hair soft on my bare arms. When lightning flickered across the walls, her curls shone so pale they were almost white. I wrapped my arms around her and thought of Thomasina and me, curled up in our bunk in St. Ives, while the waves beat against the lighthouse. My salt tears trickled into Lizzy's hair. Despite the storm, she was almost asleep again, leaning on me trustingly. Even for Thomasina, I couldn't leave her alone in this month of storms. If only Alice would come.

In the morning, we all slept late. The sun was over the horizon when Tom brought the cows into the barn. Light glimmered in the soaked grass. Flattened circles showed where the wind had hit the wheat. The maples dripped water onto the softened dirt of the driveway, and as the sun rose higher, the ground began to steam. The hills were hazy, the lake pale. In my garden, one nasturtium plant had survived the pigs. It opened flowers as yellow as butter. I picked one and stuck it into my hair as I went out to the barn to run the cream separator.

Tom was herding the cows back out again. They slipped and slid through the muddy yard. Willy was forking manure into a wagon, and ignored me as I passed. It was dim and warm and smelly in the barn.

Matthew was in one of the horse stalls, brushing his beautiful chestnut trotter. It shone like satin in the dull light. Its huge brown eyes, rimmed with white, rolled nervously and its nostrils fluttered.

"Steady now, whoa there," Matthew said. The only time his voice sounded happy was when he talked to his horses.

I poured a pail of milk into the top pan on the cream separator and began to crank the handle. Flies buzzed in the stillness, and the dog lay across the open door. Presently Matthew led the horse outside, its hooves ringing on stones. Tom appeared, quickly tacked up another horse, and led it out too. Then I glimpsed Matthew leaving, mounted on this other horse and leading the trotter on a rope.

"Off to the races," said Tom, as he came back in.

I nodded and poured another pail of milk into the separator.

"Off to gamble our sweat away," Tom continued, and I glanced at him in surprise. It wasn't like Tom to talk without being spoken to. "Horses, horses, while the fields grow couch grass and sumac, and the boy gets silly on whiskey. And you, a slip of a girl, trying to run a house. What a place." He stared gloomily at the barn floor, moving stray wisps of straw around with the toe of his boot.

"Tom," I asked hesitantly, "what do you think is the matter with Mrs. Howard?"

Tom shrugged his loose shoulders. "I dunno, Maggie. Lost the will to care about anything, maybe. Given up on this place, I shouldn't wonder."

"Would a change help her?"

"Ha! Ain't gonna to be any change around here, girl."

"But if she could —" I broke off and stopped turning the separator handle. Tom passed me with his long, shambling stride. We both had our heads cocked, listening.

"Now who can this be?" he wondered, as I came to stand beside him in the barn doorway. We watched the strange buggy rattle to a halt beside the house. The driver, a man, climbed down. Then he lifted out a slender woman. Her hat floated over her, a huge saucer heaped with flowers and feathers. The morning sun gleamed on her smooth, shining dress with its lace collar. She paused and looked around. When she saw us, she lifted one delicate arm and waved graciously. Her gloves came to her elbows.

There was only one person she could be.

CHAPTER
ELEVEN

As I crossed the yard, all I could think about was my dirty bare feet. I scuffed my toes through the wet grass, trying to wipe them clean. Tom, with his long stride, reached the buggy first.

"What can I do for you folks?" he asked.

"I'm looking for Mrs. Kathleen Howard. I'm her sister, from Toronto," said Alice. Her voice was like Kathleen's voice, but brighter, as if there was sunshine in it. She raised one hand gracefully, inside the white glove, and waved to me.

"Maggie Curnow?" she asked.

"Yes, ma'am," I answered, the way I'd been taught to in the Barnardo Home in London, when I was a small girl. I couldn't stop staring at Alice. She was like one of the ladies Mae Beth and I admired in the Hudson's Bay catalogue. Her dress gleamed with blue threads. Pink and purple ostrich plumes nodded on her blue straw hat, and her eyes sparkled at me as if we shared a secret. I tried to hunch down shorter, hoping my faded dress would cover my dirty feet.

"I'm so glad that you wrote to me, Maggie," Alice said, and then she paid the buggy driver from a thin, black leather wallet. "Come back for me tomorrow morning," she directed him. As he climbed into the buggy, I saw that it had the address of a livery stable in Peterborough painted in gold lettering on the side. It was a hired buggy.

"I'll carry this," said Tom, stooping to lift Alice's carpetbag and her hatbox. He held the door open gallantly as Alice swept into the kitchen, her dress whispering around her like summer leaves. Then Tom followed her inside, staring. I think he was as dazzled as me. After setting the carpetbag down, he lingered by the kitchen door as if hoping there was something more he could do, but Alice ignored him. She peeled her long gloves off slowly as she looked around the kitchen. I was ashamed that everything was so grubby and messy. I didn't think that Alice could possibly understand how much work there was to do in this house. She would think that I was lazy. She might scold me.

But she smiled at me instead. "And where is my sister?" she asked.

"Ummn . . . she's . . . well, I don't know if she's up yet," I mumbled. "Why don't you come sit in the parlor and I'll let her know that you're here?"

"Yes," Alice agreed, pulling out a hatpin with a glass bead on one end. She lifted the beautiful hat off, and set it on the table's shabby oilcloth. I couldn't wait to get her out of the kitchen. When I led her to the parlor, I saw that the door was open and I heard the rocking chair creaking. Kathleen was up after all.

"Your sister is here," I said.

"Kathleen?" Alice paused in the doorway, as if uncertain. The creaking of the chair stopped. "Kathleen?" Alice asked again, and then she rustled into the room, and bent over the rocking chair. "My dear! I've come to surprise you!" she exclaimed with a laugh.

At first, I thought maybe Kathleen didn't recognize her own sister. She just stared at Alice with that blank, faraway look. Then I thought maybe I had done the wrong thing; maybe Kathleen didn't want her sister here. Maybe they'd had a disagreement and maybe I was going to be in trouble for this. Suddenly, Kathleen gave a kind of gasp and a cry, then raised her arms and clung to Alice.

"It's a wonderful morning," said Alice sweetly, as she rustled over to the closed drapes and pulled them wide open.

In the bright light, I saw that Kathleen's face was wet with tears, but Alice didn't say anything about this. All she said was, "We must have breakfast together, Kathleen. You get yourself tidied up, and Maggie and I will make tea. Come on." She took Kathleen's hand and tugged.

Slowly Kathleen stood up in her faded, wrinkled old wrap and nightie. I was ashamed for her. She looked bewildered and white, and she kept crying without making any noise. "How did you get here . . . all this way?" she asked.

"Train from Toronto to Peterborough, where I took a room last night. Then a hired buggy brought me here this morning," said Alice brightly. "Now, go and put something summery on, do. I've brought some city things with me. You'll love them."

She gave Kathleen the slightest of pushes in the small of her back, and Kathleen went slowly towards the stairs.

"Let's get breakfast, Maggie," Alice said, leading the way back to the kitchen.

"Oh, that's my job," I protested. "You can't — you'll get dirty — please let me —"

But Alice was already tying an apron around her gleaming dress and humming to herself. "Tell me what to do," she said.

I didn't know what to say. Should I send her out to work the pump? Should I ask her to cook porridge? She was probably used to servants; she shouldn't have been in the kitchen. She must have read my mind.

"I'm not useless," she teased, with her sunshiny smile. I flushed, and handed her a pan. "If you make the porridge, I'll fetch more water for tea," I said.

I was happy to escape out to the pump. The handle squeaked as I worked it up and down, and water spouted into the pail in bright arcs. I wondered what was in Alice's carpetbag, and if she could make Kathleen stop crying and smile. I wondered what she could do about Lizzy, and if I would ever be free of this place. Then I carried the water inside to the dirty kitchen, where Alice was stirring porridge.

"Don't you have any piped water?" she asked, and I shook my head.

Then she wanted to know who did the cooking, who

tended the garden, who made the butter and did the chores, who cared for Lizzy, who blacked the stove and cleaned the lamps and beat the rugs and baked the bread.

"And what does my sister do?" she asked at last.

"Well, mostly she just . . . she sits in the parlor a lot. She looks at old pictures," I said.

"What else?" Alice's bright eyes flickered between the thickening porridge and my own face. She smiled encouragingly at me. "Why did you write and tell me she wasn't well, Maggie? What's wrong with her?"

"She just . . . she doesn't care about anything anymore. Maybe . . ." I trailed off.

"Maggie, you must say what you know," said Alice firmly. "I can't help unless I know the problem."

I remembered Tom's words in the barn that morning. "Maybe she's given up," I repeated boldly. "I mean, she visits the cemetery and thinks about the dead children. She doesn't care about the farm anymore. She's given up on the real world and just lives . . . lives in her memories."

I knew, as I said these words, that they were true. Her memories were the faraway place that Kathleen was always looking back at. Just the way I kept looking backwards over my shoulder, into the past I had shared with Thomasina. This thought frightened me. I didn't want to end up like Kathleen.

"Is this a good farm?" Alice asked.

"Tom says it's a poor farm because Mr. Howard doesn't care anymore either."

"Doesn't he work the farm with Willy?"

"Willy only wants to get away. He likes motorcars, not farming. And Matt — Mr. Howard — only cares about his horses and going to the races."

It felt disrespectful, talking about the Howards like this. But Alice spoke to me as if I was an adult. I kept glancing around, checking that no one was about to walk in and hear me. Then I would be in trouble for sure.

"And how is Lizzy?" Alice asked.

"Lizzy's good," I said earnestly. I wanted Alice to know that Lizzy would be easy to care for. "Lizzy's a sweet child," I said. "I take care of her . . . but I'm not always around and there's so much work to do and some-times she wanders off and I'm afraid she'll get lost or hurt, and I can't be everywhere at once —"

I broke off, horrified. My words had come tumbling out like apples from a basket. Now Alice would think I was just a child, not anywhere near being an adult, and she would stop talking to me. I pressed my hand over my mouth and stared at the floor. Alice's dress whispered across to me. I felt her hand rest lightly on my arm.

"Maggie, I'm sorry for all the questions. I just needed to know what was wrong here. I won't ask anymore. Don't be upset," she said.

I raised my eyes to her face. She was smiling. I thought that this was how Alice managed to be success-ful in life: she was bright and energetic and treated people well; she was smart and thought about things and did something about them. I wanted to be like her.

"Oh, the porridge!" cried Alice, and she rushed back to the stove and lifted the pan off. "Burned on the bottom! Don't tell anyone!" she said, and suddenly we were both laughing the way Mae Beth and I laughed at nothing much sometimes.

When Kathleen came downstairs for breakfast, she had stopped crying. I saw that she had even tried to do something about her appearance. She was wearing a gown that she used to wear for church. The cuffs were worn and two buttons were missing, but Alice praised her and told her that she looked summery. Kathleen's pale cheeks actually flushed with pleasure.

Lizzy came downstairs for breakfast too, and stared at Alice with her eyes stretched wide open. I held my breath. It was really important for Lizzy and Alice to like each other. At first Lizzy hid behind me and wouldn't let go of my skirt. Then she got bolder, and sat down to eat her smoky porridge. After breakfast, Alice opened her carpet-bag and lifted out the most beautiful doll, with a smooth porcelain face and a velvet dress. Neither Lizzy nor I had ever seen anything like it. When Alice gave it to Lizzy, Lizzy was speechless. She fingered the lace on the doll's drawers, and stroked the doll's glossy cheeks and golden hair. She sat on her Aunt Alice's knee, hugging the doll while Alice told her about her cousins in the city.

In her hatbox, Alice had a hat for Kathleen, trimmed with feathers and flowers like her own. She made Kathleen try it on. She had brought gloves for her too — which was funny, really. Where would Kathleen ever wear gloves and a fancy hat?

There were other surprises in Alice's carpetbag. She pulled out a bottle of scent with a lid cut in the shape of a flower, and dabbed scent on Lizzy's wrists. Next came a shiny box, made of something Alice called mother-of-pearl, and inside it was a cake of pink powder. She patted some onto Kathleen's pale cheeks. I had never seen face powder — Alice called it cosmetics — before. Oh, if only Mae Beth was here! It would be hard to describe all of Alice's things to her. Having Alice with us felt like having a princess in the kitchen.

Later, while I picked tomatoes and beans in the garden, the sisters sat on the verandah and looked at Kathleen's old album. I could see Kathleen wiping her eyes; she must have been crying again. The beans snapped off their runners, and I dropped them into a bushel basket. Tomorrow, I would have to can them all. The sun beat down on my bent back, but I hardly noticed it. I kept thinking about the past being like a place you could never return to, no matter how hard you tried. Kathleen could never be that person beside the lake again, that girl in her old album. Thomasina and I could never be those little girls who had run on the beach in St. Ives. I tried to imagine what it would be like, when we met each other . . . I hoped we could be friends.

When the sun was overhead, I went in to cook some lunch. Then I tiptoed down the hall and lingered just inside the verandah door, where I could hear the sisters talking. I knew this was sneaky, but I had to know if Alice was going to do anything. The first noise I heard was Kathleen, sniffling.

Then Alice said, "The driver's coming back in the morning. I'll help you get ready."

"It's such a long way to go," lamented Kathleen.

"No, it's not far. You'll enjoy the change of scene. And it's not right that Lizzy doesn't know her cousins," said Alice in her firm, bright voice. I could see how she managed a big house with servants.

"You'd like to meet your cousins, wouldn't you, Lizzy?" Alice asked. "They have a nursery with a rocking horse to ride on, and a whole box full of dolls."

"My doll's called Lily," said Lizzy suddenly, and I smothered a nervous giggle in the dim hallway.

"I don't have any money," protested Kathleen. "I can't come."

"Oh, Kathleen. I told you that Roland has been appointed Queen's Council. I have quite enough money to buy you a ticket to Toronto. We'll pack your bags this afternoon."

"Matthew won't like it," Kathleen said.

"I'll talk to him," responded Alice, and then I heard the rustle of her dress as she stood up. "It must be time for lunch," she said, and I fled back down the hall on tiptoe. In the kitchen I hugged myself tight, with both arms. My plan was working! Alice was going to take Kathleen and Lizzy away to the city, where they would be cared for, and I would be free to leave and find Thomasina.

At lunch, when Willy slouched in, Alice ignored his glowering stare, just the way she ignored his bony elbows on the table, and the way he chewed with his mouth open. I noticed that Tom had washed his face at the pump, and slicked his hair back with water, and I smiled to myself and wondered if Alice had noticed too.

I didn't think there was much that Alice didn't notice.

In the afternoon, the sisters sat on the verandah again, and Alice told stories about people they both knew in the city. Lizzy played with her doll. She sang Cornish hymns to it, the ones I had sung to her at bedtime. I had been so busy planning how to get Lizzy sent away that it had never occurred to me, until now, that I might miss her. I started thinking about Thomasina again, wondering if she had missed me all these years. Then I ran out to the barn and asked Tom to kill a chicken for a special supper.

He killed two and plucked them both, and all I had to do was put them in the oven to roast. I washed beans and husked corn, and put potatoes on to boil. I wanted the meal to feel like a celebration, because I knew that big changes were coming and that I, Maggie Curnow, had helped make them happen.

Matthew Howard came home just in time for supper, with his two horses. When he strode into the kitchen, he didn't seem surprised to see Alice there. He just stared at her with his heavy, flat eyes and sat down to cut up the chicken on its oval platter.

Alice didn't let this bother her. She told him that Roland sent his greetings, and she inquired after the day's horse race. Matthew ate with his mouth open, just like Willy, and grunted answers. Later, when I was washing the dishes, Alice asked Matthew if she could talk to him in the parlor. I snuck down the hall, dripping water on the floor, and listened outside the door.

". . . do her good. She needs a change of scene," Alice was saying.

There was a dull, brooding silence, then Matthew said, "A woman's place is at home with her family."

"Of course it is," agreed Alice cleverly. "But a little change doesn't hurt, and when she comes home again, she might be much better. She's not well, Matthew."

Matthew grunted, then sighed. "You ladies must do as you think best," he muttered. Then he warned crossly, "But don't you go fillin' her head with city notions. She's a farmer's wife now. I don't care what she was when she was growin' up like a little princess. She's got used to plain ways now. Don't you go meddlin' with that."

"I just want her to have a rest," said Alice soothingly.

Matthew grunted again, then I heard his heavy step move towards the parlor door, and I scampered back to my pan of dirty dishes.

That night, when Lizzy went to bed, I told her all her favorite stories, even though I was tired. I sang to her until she fell asleep, with her doll clasped tightly against her chest. Its golden hair was even brighter than Lizzy's own. "Goodbye, Lizzy," I whispered, and kissed her on the cheek softly, so as not to waken her.

After breakfast the next morning, Tom carried all the bags and cases outside and piled them by the edge of the driveway. In the kitchen, Alice was helping Kathleen pin her new hat on. When Kathleen hugged Willy goodbye, she started crying again and Willy went stiff as a poker and stared at his boots. I heard him cussing beneath his breath, and his father must have heard too because he glared at his son.

"Willy, you and Tom need to fix that fence at the

bottom of the barley field," Matthew ordered. "The cattle will be in the crop. And Tom, saddle up the mare. I'm off to see McTavish about the threshing crew."

"Yes," said Tom, and he and Willy clomped out and headed for the barn.

"Maggie, you've got canning to do. Beans and tomatoes. Wash the jars first," Matthew told me.

"Yes," I said.

"I'll expect you home soon," said Matthew to Kathleen, as he rose from the breakfast table. "Don't forget where your place is."

"Yes, no," said Kathleen nervously, her eyes jumping around under the hat. Only Alice was serene. "She'll write you a letter," she told Matthew. "You'll hear something soon."

Matthew nodded curtly, and followed the others out to the barn. Soon, while Kathleen sniffled in a chair and Alice and I did the dishes, we heard the mare trot away. I knew that Matthew would be gone for hours. The next sound we heard was the hired buggy arriving, and we went outside and stood by the cases. "Whoa there," the driver called, and climbed down to load the luggage.

Kathleen peered at me from under the hat's sweeping brim, looking worried. "Can you cook all the meals for the men while I'm away?" she asked.

"Yes," I muttered, thinking that she must have been asleep for the last few months, while I had cooked for everyone. I watched as the driver handed Kathleen into the buggy, and swung Lizzy in beside her.

"Maggie," said Alice, with her hand on my arm,

"you're a good, hardworking girl. Thank you for taking care of everyone. If you ever need anything, Maggie, contact me. You know my address and I want you to think of me as a friend."

Then, with her gloved hand, she pressed the glass bottle of scent into my own hand, and swished away to the buggy.

Lizzy made her doll wave at me, and she giggled with excitement. "Going to the city, Maggie!" she shrilled, even though she didn't know what a city was.

I stood watching as the buggy rolled away between the maple trees. The women's feathers nodded in the breeze. At the gate, Lizzy stood up and waved her doll's hand again. Then the horse turned onto the road, and trotted away. In the sudden silence, a robin sang.

I went into the house and pulled the bushel basket of beans out of the pantry, where it had sat all night. Then I began carrying the glass sealer jars into the kitchen and lining them up on the table. I kept imagining Alice and Kathleen in the city; I wanted to think about Kathleen looking young and happy again, and laughing in that sunshiny way that Alice did. The house seemed very quiet.

Suddenly, I understood — this was my chance!

Now, *right now*, while the men were outside and busy, while the women were traveling — this was my chance to run away. If the men came home for lunch and found the house empty, they would think that I had gone to Toronto with the women. And the women wouldn't even know I was missing; they would think I was still on the farm cooking for the men.

My stomach lurched. For a long moment I stood perfectly still, staring at the sunlight reflected in the glass jars. I took a long breath, and suddenly I sprang into action. I ran up the stairs, panting, and pulled the flour sack from the closet. Into it I packed my best dress, a clean apron, my three seashells, Alice's bottle of scent, Harold's two dollars. I laced my hot feet into my tight boots. In the pantry, I took a loaf of bread and some cheese, almost half a cold chicken, four tomatoes, some spice cake. I placed the food on top of the apron in my bag. I filled a sealer jar at the pump, and screwed the lid on tight. It seemed heavy but I had to have water, so I carried it into the kitchen and snuggled it into the bottom of my bag. I slung the bag over my shoulder, and glanced around. Dust hung in sunbeams. The stove was warm, but I knew the fire inside was low. By the time the men came in for lunch, there would be only ashes left.

I went down the verandah steps, because I liked this side of the house and I wanted to say goodbye to it. I picked a nasturtium flower off the only plant left, and tucked it into a buttonhole. Then I looked all around, but couldn't see or hear Willy or Tom. I imagined them down near the lake, struggling with cedar posts and wire.

I began to walk down the drive. I wouldn't look back. I wouldn't run. I kept each stride the same length. I was sweating.

When I had walked as far as the railway cutting, I switched the flour bag to my other shoulder and started to breathe normally. I reached the place where Willy had jumped out of the bushes at me, but this time the grass

was empty. Only my shadow moved, and small birds
fluttered in the shimmering air. The wind smelled like
ripe grain. Once I glimpsed men stooking barley, far off
in a field, but they didn't pay any attention to me. When
the sun was high in the northern sky, I sat under a bush
and ate a tomato. My mouth was too dry to eat bread or
cake. I had three mouthfuls of water, and took my boots
off to look at my blisters. Then I started walking again.

In three days, I would be with Thomasina

CHAPTER
TWELVE

When I first woke up, I didn't know where I was. Pale light filtered through the cracks between weathered boards; the lines of light were crooked and thin. I opened my eyes wider. Then I remembered. I was in the loft of a barn, curled in the nest of hay I had made the previous evening. I was in a back corner, where I hoped no one would find me. When I got my eyes wide open, I found a ginger and white barn cat sitting on a beam and staring at me. It had long whiskers and round, golden eyes.

From below me came muffled sounds: the ring of a bucket on a hard floor, an occasional word spoken in a man's voice, the low mooing of cows. It must be milking time, I thought. I would have to keep still and wait. Presently the cat yawned, then walked away along the beam on tiptoe. I wondered if it ever fell off, and I remembered all the cats in St. Ives that had walked wherever they pleased: along roof ridges and back fences, the tops of walls, the gunwales of boats. They never fell.

While I waited for the milking to be finished, I opened my flour bag cautiously, and had a drink of water and a piece of cheese. My stomach rumbled hungrily as I chewed. My legs were already aching, and I hadn't even started on all the walking I would have to do today. I looked ruefully at my feet and wished I had something to wrap around the blisters. As I ate, the light shining through the cracks in the barn wall grew brighter and stronger. Presently I heard the door squeak open, then the man's voice saying, "Get on then, girls. Get out."

I slid across the hay to the wall and pressed my eye to the crack — the cows' splotchy backs swayed beneath me as they walked to the fields. Presently the farmer walked through my view too. Then there was silence. I waited for what seemed like a long time before I slipped quickly down the ladder and out the barn door. In only a minute, I was over the fence and onto the railway lane.

Soon, I would be in Peterborough.

Dew shimmered on the grass. Once I glimpsed a red fox trotting across the path ahead of me. His bushy tail blazed like a candle flame. I found red apples hanging in a tree and I put several in my flour bag, and one in each pocket. They were hard and tangy, but sweet. Birds called and a horse neighed somewhere. The aches stretched out of my legs. Yellow goldenrod swayed in the breeze.

I'm free, I thought, *free! free!*

Nobody in the whole world knew where I was. I was finally going to do what I had needed to do for years: find my twin again. My heart pounded fast when I thought about meeting Thomasina. There was so much we would have to tell each other!

I walked along grinning and spitting out apple seeds and swinging my flour bag. Presently, the ground in front of me began to fall away in a long sweep of green. I paused in the shade and stared into the wide valley below. The spires and chimneys of Peterborough broke through a surface of billowing trees.

I hadn't been to Peterborough for years, although when I first lived at the farm the Howards occasionally went there in the buggy, taking me along too. Now I felt nervous about walking through so many streets, and being looked at by so many strangers. I lifted my flour bag onto my shoulder and began to descend the rolling hills.

When I came to the first houses, I tried not to rush past them. I reminded myself that no one knew I was a runaway, and no one cared about where I was going or what I was doing. When a woman hanging out laundry glanced my way, I gave her a cheery wave. I wondered if I looked funny, walking on the railway line. Maybe I should walk along the roads instead.

The next street was called Wolsely and I headed down it, carrying my flour bag bundled up in one hand. Dogs and cats watched me. Two girls, about Lizzy's age, played on some front steps. A man passed me, balancing a plank on one shoulder. A horse and buggy rattled by at a trot. Wolsely was heading the wrong way; I knew I should be going southwards but the sun on my back told me I was heading west. Soon I found another road, called Benson, which was going south. I went down it with the sun on my left cheek.

And then I saw it. My dream house.

I leaned on the cedar fence, listening to bees buzzing in the flowers. I breathed perfume deep into my lungs. The house was sided with wooden boards, and painted the gray-blue color of stones. On the front verandah stood a round wicker table and two white chairs. Blue shutters flanked every window. Climbing roses twined around the shutters, and the blue trumpets of morning glories smothered the outside of the verandah. Sweet peas climbed the fence where I leaned. Sunflowers lifted their heavy heads towards the sun. Marigolds shone closer to the ground. It was as if my little garden on the farm had been reborn again, bigger and better than ever.

Oh, imagine living here! I thought. I leaned on the fence for a long time, while the bees buzzed and the horse in the barn hung his head over the door and gazed at me. He had a white blaze, and his barn was made of the same blue boards as the house. Lilac bushes crowded against the barn walls, and a snowball bush stood by the yard's front gate.

Finally, I walked on. All the way down Benson, and then going eastwards on Smith Street, I thought about the house and its beautiful garden. I wondered who lived there, and who grew the flowers. I wondered if I would ever have a garden like that.

When I found another street going south, I turned onto it. Presently I found a sign telling me I was on George Street. I passed a planing mill, where saws whined like angry hornets, then a tall church with a square tower. When I saw a park with bright flowers blooming, I walked across the grass and bent down to smell them. After this, George Street became full of hurrying people, horses, wagons, buggies. A tall, brick tower held a clock, and the pavements were lined with stores. I stared into the windows as I passed. In butcher shops, white chickens hung by their yellow feet, and huge slabs of beef dripped blood onto the sawdust floors. One window held chocolates arranged in gold and purple boxes. My stomach growled. I passed a hotel where I glimpsed a lobby carpeted in red, and potted plants lined up against the wall. Bread steamed gently in bakeries, where I gazed at doughnuts and cherry tarts and lemon pies. I thought of my two dollars, but I knew I mustn't spend it yet, not while I still had food in my bag.

At Lechs The Furriers, I stared at gleaming coats and beaver muffs, and imagined being rich enough to own one. Maybe Alice had a fur coat. I looked for a flower shop, but I didn't see one. Colored awnings above the shop windows cast rectangles of shadow over me as I walked.

The town was full of people, all bustling about their day's business. Boys in sailor suits ran after their mothers. Men raised their Homburg hats politely to ladies. Delivery boys whistled jauntily, and delivery wagons rattled up and down the dirt street; *Fannings Laundry*, *Fielding The Grocer*, *Stocks Bread*, I read on some of them. Dairy wagons delivered milk, and the air was filled with the sound of hooves trotting, people calling, doors closing, saws whining.

At first I was afraid to look at the people, in case someone looked back too hard and guessed my secret. I kept expecting a hand to grab me by the shoulder and spin me around, for a voice to tell me I was being sent back to the farm. But no one paid any attention to me. Presently, I forgot to worry. Then I stared at ladies with flouncing skirts, little girls with frilled pinafores, and men with soft beards and pale summer suits. I imagined that I lived here in the town; that I had a mother like Alice; that I was out to do some shopping. I went down George Street with my eyes stretched wide open and darting everywhere, and my head in a spin. Town was so exciting!

Finally, I reached the end of the shops, and I went on southwards past a lake surrounded by factories, where the air smelled of strange, acrid chemicals. I wrinkled my nose and hurried my steps until I was amongst houses again. It seemed to be taking me forever to get through this town, but when the houses thinned and the fields began, I wondered which way I should go to find Keene. I couldn't picture the maps in Miss Hooper's house anymore; when I shut my eyes all I could see were flowers and shop windows. I wondered if I should stop at a house and ask directions, but I was afraid of the questions I might be asked in return. If people knew I was a runaway, what would they do with me?

I stood at the roadside, resting my feet and trying to decide what to do, when along came the strangest thing I had ever seen: a huge, rolling wheel with a frame joining it to a tiny back wheel. On top, high against the bright sky, a man perched on a narrow seat. His feet spun around on pedals, and his gangly thin legs moved up and down.

"Good morning, miss," he greeted me, lifting his straw hat with one hand. As he did so, the contraption he was riding veered alarmingly. I thought he was going to fall into the ditch, but his body swerved in perfect balance and brought the wheels back under control. He did this without seeming to notice. His green eyes twinkled at me from under his hat brim.

"Morning, sir," I replied politely.

"Are you lingering to imbibe the day's beauty, or because you have lost your way?" he inquired, riding a circle in the middle of the road as he spoke.

"I'm wondering which is the way to Keene," I answered boldly. If he wanted to know more, I would have to think up a story quickly.

"To Keene? On the shores of the delectable, sparkling Rice Lake?" he called over his shoulder, as he executed another circle in the road.

I began to smile. There was something odd about him. "To Keene," I repeated. When he turned to face me again, he nodded in a friendly way, and ran a hand over his red mustache. The wheels wobbled. I saw that his freckles were the same color as mine.

"Allow me, young lady . . . allow me to escort you towards the fair village of Keene. We are on the right road. Will you give me the pleasure of your company?"

I couldn't tell if he was teasing me. I watched as he circled again, but when the circle was completed, I nodded.

"Wonderful. Splendid. And from what part of Home do you hail?"

"Home?" I asked. Now it was time for my story, or he would know that I was a runaway.

"The motherland, the Queen of the Empire — England, my dear miss. Or am I mistaken about your charming accent?"

"Well no, that is, I'm from Cornwall," I replied.

His pale skin flushed, his freckles glowed. He lifted his straw hat and swung it through the air in an arc while the sun flamed in his red hair. "Cornwall! A jewel in the crown! Home of humble fisherfolk and staunch hearts! A paradise of light and color!" he cried.

He almost fell off his contraption at this point, while I stared in astonishment.

Suddenly I began to giggle. "Have you been there?" I asked.

"Been there? I have lived there! In the most quaint, charming, higgeldy piggeldy town of St. Ives! I am an artist, dear miss — and St. Ives is saturated with light, with subject matter, with crooked cottages and white sand and mournful donkeys. Oh, St. Ives was ecstasy, a feast for the soul!"

I was standing like a statue. He brought his contraption around in a circle and peered at me. "Are you quite well?" he asked.

"St. Ives," I whispered. "Sir, it was my home."

"Extraordinary, by George! But, surely, no mere coincidence. There are more things in heaven and earth, Horatio, than are dreamt of in your philosophy," he said solemnly. Then, in one nimble move, he sprang onto the road in his tweed knickerbockers and his cream-colored socks, his fine linen shirt and his dusty leather shoes. He took my hand.

"William Frances Angus MacCallum Archer, at your service, miss. My mother was a MacCallum who married a Sassenach. This is a meeting of Celts, a meeting of significance. You may call me Archie," he said graciously, bending over my hand.

"I'm Maggie," I replied.

"Maggie of the fisherfolk," he mused, still holding my hand. Then he remembered, and let it go. "Have you any provisions for this arduous road to Keene?" he asked. "It must be high time for a little taste of something. Shall we sit?" He indicated the grass with a sweep of his hat, and I sat down.

"What is that thing?" I asked, as he laid his set of wheels gently beside us.

"This is a penny-farthing bicycle. This is freedom, silence, the open road, my dear. I cannot abide horses; they are all yellow teeth and loud noises. My father rode to hounds in Wiltshire," the man replied. Archie. I had to call him that.

From the pack on his back, Archie took out some ham sandwiches made of white bread with no crusts. Although I told him I had chicken, he insisted I eat a sandwich. He poured me tea from a flask, and handed me a wedge of fruitcake. He showed me his sketch pad and his little blocks of watercolor paints — their brightness made me think of flowers. I told him about my garden at the farm, and how Willy wrecked it with the pigs.

Archie looked solemn and grasped my hand again. "Maggie," he said, "the important gardens are the ones you carry *here*, inside you." He thumped himself dramatically on his skinny chest.

"What do you mean?"

"In here, you carry your visions, your heart full of hope and flowers. No one can spoil it, Maggie. It is your gift. You can grow flowers anywhere you go. You will have other gardens."

He gave my hand a squeeze, as if we were old friends. Then he took another bite of sandwich and started to talk about St. Ives, about high and low tide, about Porth Meor beach and the studio he had beside a sail loft.

"Why did you leave St. Ives?" I asked.

"It's in here," he replied mysteriously, thumping his chest again. "It's the wanderlust, it's the Celt in me. I have to see new horizons, new skies. Everywhere you go in the world, the light is different. Absolutely different! Can you believe it?" he asked in astonishment. "I have dedicated my life to the light."

"Where's your family?" I asked.

He looked momentarily gloomy. "In England, in the bosom of Wiltshire," he replied. "My father is a Lord and my mother is a Lady. I am the eldest son, a profligate and a black sheep," he said. "And where is your family?"

I told him about Thomasina, and about us being orphans. I had decided I could trust him, although he was unlike any person I had ever met.

After lunch, he put his pack on his back and mounted his penny-farthing. "Young Celtic queen, I salute you," he said, and he saluted like a soldier, but he wasn't exactly teasing. "I am currently living in Peterborough," he said. "If you ever need assistance, I will be honored to assist you. God speed you to Keene." He flung out an arm and pointed southwards, wobbled impressively, then rode away with light spinning on his wheels. He seemed to have forgotten about escorting me anywhere.

After that, I walked for hours without seeing anyone except for a man with a wagonload of logs, and a boy herding cattle. The boy had no shirt, and torn pants, and a big stick in one hand. He was almost as small as Lizzy, and the cattle had curved horns and rough coats. "Where you going?" the boy asked me, and "Keene," I replied. When I turned and looked back, he was staring after me with round eyes.

Late in the afternoon, I heard wagon wheels behind me and I stopped by the side of the road. First came three skinny dogs, trotting with their tails between their legs and their tongues hanging out. Then came two boys about my age, wearing strange black hats with floppy brims. Their faces were dark brown and their eyes were almost black. They stared at me but didn't speak. Behind them came three wagons, pulled by tired horses. Flies hung in clouds around their heads. Canvas, stretched over round frames, covered the wagons. Faces of children and women peered out from underneath it. Silent, dark men drove the first two wagons. The third wagon was driven by a woman.

I began to walk again, following the wagons. After some time, the woman riding in the last one patted the back boards with her hand, and pointed at me. Then she pointed at the wagon again. I walked faster. I pointed at myself, then at the wagon, and the woman smiled. Why didn't she speak? I swung myself up onto the wagon, and finally the woman said something but I couldn't understand it. She was speaking a different language, and the sounds were harsh and sloping in her mouth, like jagged pieces of rock. I shrugged at her.

"You — travel *messze*?" she asked.

I shrugged again.

"*Messze, messze*? Long road?" she asked.

Oh! I smiled and nodded, and laid my head on my hands like someone sleeping. Maybe she would understand I had been traveling since yesterday. She nodded. As the wagon jolted along, she and the three girls stared at me and I stared back. They all had dark hair plaited in long braids which hung down below their belts. Their wide skirts were woven from many different colors, and bright scarves were knotted around their heads. Copper and silver discs swung at the hems of the scarves, and bracelets of silver jangled at the women's wrists. Even the little girls wore bangles. Bright ribbons streamed from the girls' hair, and long strings of glass beads hung from the women's necks. Their nails were dirty and their boots were worn.

Finally, we got tired of staring solemnly at each other, and the woman and the driver began talking together in their harsh words. I relaxed slowly against the rolled blankets, while the wagon swayed southwards. I was glad to rest my sore feet, but I was a little scared too. I remembered Mae Beth telling me about the gypsies, and her mother had said they couldn't be trusted. They were dirty and nasty, she'd said. I imagined her horror if she could see me now, riding in a gypsy wagon. Suddenly I felt daring and free, and I smiled to myself. One of the little girls smiled back at me, her eyes as bright and dark as a chipmunk's. I began to think about Thomasina again. How her blue eyes would sparkle when she saw me! How surprised she would be!

The sun was setting. The hills were hazy and golden. Cedar trees cast their shadows and their fragrance across the road. The gypsy wagons stopped by a wooden pipe, where spring water gurgled into a trough. The women jumped out and unharnessed the horses and hobbled their feet. The children gathered firewood.

I wondered what to do. It was almost dark. I couldn't see any barns for me to sleep in. I didn't know if the gypsies wanted me to stay with them, and I began to feel scared again in the bottom of my stomach. In the last light, the gypsies were mysterious figures, full of glinting teeth and swinging jewelry. I began to walk away. Suddenly the woman who had been driving the wagon caught me by the arm. She pointed to her mouth, to her stomach, to me. "*Eszik, eszik*. Food," she said. When she tugged my arm, I turned back to the wagons. The men stared at me curiously. I sat by the road and waited to see what would happen.

When the fires were lit, the women set up black cooking pots, and made flat bread and stew. I pulled my chicken from my bag, and gave some of it to the little girls who sat watching me. The dogs came sniffing by, and one of them grabbed my loaf of bread as fast as a fish jumping for bait. One of the boys kicked the dog as it ran past him, and it yelped. Soon I could hear all the dogs fighting in the road. It was dark now. The gypsies swirled around the fire in their swinging skirts, their clinking bangles. A horse snorted. The fire crackled and people ate, sucking on their fingers, crunching bones. A coyote howled and I was glad to be near a fire.

After supper, one of the men pulled a mouth organ from his pocket. He played mournful tunes, and the two women danced and swayed in the flickering light, their worn-out boots shuffling the dirt into ridges. I thought that it must have been getting very late. Smoke filled my head. Finally everyone went back to the wagons, and the women rolled out the blankets. "*Alszik*," one woman said to me, laying her head on her hands to mimic sleep. I lay down in the last wagon, with one of the women and the three little girls. It was so quiet late at night that I thought I could hear the dew falling.

In the morning, I rode with the gypsies until they turned off on another road, and then I walked on alone to Keene. I waved when the last wagon pulled out of sight, and the little girls waved back. "*Istenhozzad*!" the woman called out; maybe she was saying goodbye or good luck. You were wrong, I told Mae Beth's mother in my thoughts. The gypsies aren't nasty, and they wear beautiful skirts and silver rings.

As the sun rose high in the sky, I reached Keene, with its cemetery and maple trees, its brick houses and general store. It was a small place. I went into the store and asked how to find the Smiths' farm. "Out on Settler's Line," replied the plump woman behind the counter. "Three miles east of here to the Line. Then head north. Second farm on the left hand side." I felt her eyes on my back as I went out.

Another three miles! My legs ached; I thought of Thomasina. What would I say when I met her? Would she know me? How could she not know me? I turned east and went on walking. I didn't want to stop for lunch, so I ate as I walked along. My chicken was all gone and so were my tomatoes. I took bites of apple and bites of cheese and chewed them up together. Then I had a drink from my jar, which I had filled at the spring with the gypsies. Settler's Line was a dirt road heading north over the hills. I bent forward from the waist and climbed the first hill slowly, stopping to rest halfway up it. When I looked back, I saw a brilliant blue lake amongst the curving hills. Maybe it was Archie's Rice Lake; maybe he had painted pictures of it.

The late afternoon sun was heavy on my back. I went over the top of the hill and into the shade on the other side. My feet skidded in the dirt. Sugar maples and cottonwoods bent over the road. Soon, soon I would see Thomasina. Maybe when I knocked on the farmhouse door, she would be the person who opened it. What would I say to her? What would she say to me?

I passed a sugar shack and a pond where white geese swam lazily. They cackled as I passed, stretching out their necks. I passed the first farm, then saw the second one set above the road on a hilltop. The wooden house and ramshackle barns leaned against the sky. I went slowly up the lane. My heart was bursting.

Thomasina, I thought. Thomasina, I'm coming.

A black and white collie dog ran out to meet me, barking loudly and waving its feathery tail. But I wasn't afraid; I told it to be quiet. I walked to the house with long, firm steps and knocked loudly on the door and held my breath. The afternoon held *its* breath. The birds were silent. The fields glowed in the sun. The trees stood still. Then there was the sound of footsteps. The door jerked open.

"*You*? What do you want around here?" the woman asked. She was heavy and big, with greasy hair and white skin like raw dough. Her jaw was square, and her teeth were big and square like horse's teeth. She wiped her rough, red hands on her dirty apron as she glared at me.

"I'm looking for Thomasina. My twin, my twin sister," I said.

The woman's eyes bored into me. "What kind of foolery is this? Ain't you Thomasina?" she asked.

"No, I'm Maggie, her twin. Is she here?"

"No, she ain't here," the woman said angrily. "And I never heard nothin' about no twin, though I can see you're the spittin' image of her."

"But they said she was working here."

"Yeah, she was here. But she weren't no good. We sent her back," the woman said.

There was the sudden sound of crying inside the house, and a child's voice called, "Ma, Ma, he's hitting me!"

"You shut up your hollering," the woman yelled over her shoulder.

"Where did Thomasina go?" I asked. "I have to find her."

"I told you, we sent her back. Stupid it was, sendin' a slip of a girl to a farm like this. We've asked for a lad instead. I don't want to see her again, or you either. Get goin' now. I've work to do." Suddenly she grabbed the door in her thick fingers and closed it in my face. I watched it swing shut as if it was moving in slow motion. I felt the blood run down through my body, like the tide going out.

When I stumbled back down the hill, I was cold and shaking all over.

C H A P T E R
T H I R T E E N

Sun spread across the dusty road in long, golden fingers.
On cranberry bushes, clusters of red berries flared into
brilliance, like glass beads. Goldenrod flowers draped
their feathery yellow sprays beneath the sumacs and
cedars. My feet trudged through the dust. My blisters
were forgotten, my legs numb with tiredness. I didn't
think about anything.

I just walked.

Crickets shrilled in the yellow grass. The road went
on and on, up hills and down hills. It was heading north.
I didn't know where exactly and I didn't care either.

I just walked.

My stomach was a tight knot of hunger, and sometimes it grumbled, but I ignored it. I had eaten my last
apple and piece of cheese, and now my food was all gone.
The shadows turned deep and blue beneath the trees,
and the birds fell silent. Cows watched me curiously
from behind a cedar snake fence; their gusty breath
sounded loud in the evening air. I didn't speak to them,
and when I passed a farm lane, I didn't even glance up it

towards the house. The last sun slipped away from me, and only the sugar maples held it in their top branches. Then it fell below the horizon and the western sky glowed a dull golden rose. The air turned blue. An early bat swooped ahead of me. I knew that I should find somewhere to spend the night, but I didn't care.

Nothing mattered anymore. I was all alone in the bottom of my deep, deep well of sadness.

Beneath the trees, it was almost black now, but I could see all right in the darkness. The road was a pale ribbon ahead of me and I kept walking. An owl called. A little animal scuttled through the leaves by the roadside. Near the top of a hill, I noticed a sugar shack standing amongst the maple trees, and I climbed over the fence and went across to it. The door was bolted, but not locked. I went inside cautiously, listening to the silence. Then I lay down against one wall, and put my flour bag under my head. It was thin and flat. My feet throbbed in my boots, and I sat up again and pulled them off. My tired fingers fumbled in the laces. I squeezed my eyes tightly shut when I lay down, trying to keep out pictures of the farm woman with her square teeth biting off words. *Sent her back . . . not here . . . no good . . . get goin' . . . get goin'.*

I pressed my eyes into the flour sack, but I could still see her, still hear her words. I had failed. Thomasina had gone back to England, along that thin white thread in the ocean. I had come too late. Maybe I would never find her again, never come this close to her.

In the morning, I awoke late and stumbled out of the

sugar shack with stiff legs. I had a drink of water for breakfast, and then I headed north again along Settler's Line. Once my stiffness passed, walking wasn't too bad. Then it began to grow hot. My head throbbed. My thoughts went silent. I stared at my boots as they swung hypnotically forward and back beneath the hem of my skirt. When they got too heavy to wear, I tied their laces together and carried them over my shoulder.

I had another drink of water — it was almost all gone. Once a buggy passed me, rattling along fast behind a flashy chestnut horse with white socks. The driver didn't stop. Another time, a threshing crew went by, heading south with their black, lumbering steam engine, their grins and whistles and jokes, their rolled-up shirt sleeves. For miles afterwards, the road was marked with the patterns of the engine's heavy steel wheels. In the middle of the afternoon, I drank my last water. In the early evening, I found a field of uncut wheat and I pulled the heads from the stems and munched on kernels of grain. Then I crawled into the wheat and lay down with a view of the pale, milky sky.

When I awoke in the night, the view was of stars. Later, the sky was pale pink and pearly as a seashell. I couldn't sleep anymore, so I started walking again, with my boots and my bag over my shoulders.

The bear was around the first bend in the road, a dark, shaggy figure sitting up in the grass and eating from a cranberry bush. I stopped and held my breath. The bear went on eating. Silently, feeling the way with my toes, I backed away until I was at the bend in the road. Then

I sat down to wait. The bear ate for a long time. The sun came up and turned its black fur to brown. Finally, it dropped to its paws and ambled away across the fields. I waited until it had been gone for a long time before rushing past the cranberry bush.

Later, a deer and her fawn skittered across the road. Later still, I heard the whine of saws and smelled fresh wood, and I knew there must be a mill in the trees. Soon a man passed with a wagonload of oak logs. He stared hard at me, and I hurried past without speaking. His brown hound dog stopped to sniff my hands before slouching on in the wagon tracks.

The air was growing hotter and very still. Sweat prickled all over me. Sullen, dark clouds were piling up along the horizon and the light was changing. I stumbled on into the afternoon, into the muttering sound of thunder, until I reached another road running east to west. I didn't know what road it was, but it seemed to be a wider, more important road than the one I had been on. My feet turned onto it, heading west.

I tried to think what to do. Should I try and reach Toronto, and get a job with good wages? Should I look for Alice and Kathleen? Or head for Peterborough, and find a job there? Maybe I should locate the gypsies again, and run away with them. I even wondered about going back to the Howards', but I knew that was a stupid idea.

I couldn't think properly. I couldn't see Miss Hooper's maps in my head. Toronto seemed a million miles away, and here I was on a road that I didn't even know the name of. I was too hot and tired and stunned to reach

Toronto. Anyway, I didn't care. I didn't care where I went. From the bottom of my dark hole, everything looked impossible.

My head throbbed, and the hills floated dizzily around me. My tongue seemed to be swelling up bigger and bigger, pushing my teeth apart. I kept imagining my sealer jar full of water, but I knew it was empty inside my flour bag. Only my feet worked well and kept swinging along.

Sometimes buggies rattled past, and wagons with logs or farm machinery perched on them. I stayed on the side of the road and kept my head down. Once, someone called something out to me, but I didn't look up or answer. I just wanted to be left alone. The road seemed to sway ahead of me. Thunder rumbled close by, and lightning flickered over the hills. The first heavy, warm drop of rain landed on my cheek.

Soon it was pouring down, and the drops no longer felt warm. My thin dress was plastered onto my back. Rain lashed my eyes, filled them with blurred, under-water images of shaggy trees and hills rolling like waves. Mud coated my toes and splashed up onto my dress. Water ran down the side of the road in pale ribbons, and the dark sky pressed down on me and the dripping flour sack and dark boots I carried. Water ran over my lips and I opened my mouth to let it fall in.

Finally I sat under some ironwood trees, waiting for the storm to pass. I was shivering when at last I took to the road again. The sun came out, and the ground steamed. Mist rose from a swamp's green water. A blue heron took off with a creaking cry when it saw me. I wrung the water from the hem of my dress, and from my sleeves, and kept walking, while the sun faded again as the evening came in soft and humid.

Suddenly, I staggered. My knees were like rubber. I regained my balance, but now I wasn't walking — I was floating down the road, floating I didn't know where — and it didn't matter. Nothing did. I was beyond pain, beyond thought. Then I staggered again, stumbling forward. My boots thumped me in the chest. I pitched into the damp grass by the road and sat there with my head hanging between my knees. The crickets were in my ears, talking to me. I didn't listen. I didn't care. I sank down into whirling darkness.

Time went by, maybe just a little time or maybe a big piece of it.

A voice started talking to me. "Maggie! Maggie! Please, I implore you. Are you ill?" The voice kept on inside my head, just like the crickets. When a warm hand shook me, stars swirled in my eyes. I wanted the voice and the hand to go away and leave me alone. Why wouldn't they stop? I shrugged my shoulder, and finally I raised my head and squinted into the twilight.

A man's worried green eyes stared into mine. "Maggie," the voice said again when the man's mouth moved. "Maggie, we mustn't linger. It will soon be dark, and you're not well. I fear you're not well at all. Can you stand?"

The man tugged on my arm. I pulled away. "Leave me alone," I muttered but he kept tugging. Archie — that's who it is, I thought stupidly. My thoughts trickled through my mind one word at a time.

"I implore you," he said again, and I tried to please him, I tried to stand. I swayed to and fro, like a tree in the wind, and leaned against his chest. He was wearing something smooth and silky which smelled of cologne. I could hear his voice vibrating in his bony ribs.

"My dear," he kept saying, in distress. "My dear miss, my dear child. Can you walk?"

"Dunno," I mumbled. "I've been walking for days, Archie. She's gone. Thomasina is gone."

"Hush, hush now," he said soothingly, the way I used to say it to Lizzy. Then he began talking to himself in an agitated murmur. "I must get assistance, immediately, without further delay. Perhaps — no, that wouldn't work. I shall fetch us a conveyance. Yes, that's the ticket."

He led me further away from the road, and propped me up against a tree trunk. "Maggie, you must remain here. I am going immediately to hire a conveyance at the livery stable. Please do not move until I return. Promise me?"

I nodded wearily. I couldn't have gone anywhere even if I had wanted to. The slightest movement made my head spin, and my skin felt hot. Chills trembled up and down my spine and my legs throbbed painfully. I heard the wheels of Archie's penny-farthing hiss away into the dusk, and then I sank down again into my dark grief.

Presently, I heard hooves and buggy wheels, and then Archie's voice calling me. He lifted me by the armpits and I staggered beside him to the buggy waiting in the darkness. Its lanterns cast pools of light over the horse's dark hindquarters, over the leather seats and the glinting harness buckles. Archie lifted me in, then climbed up beside me and chirruped to the horse.

"Yellow teeth," I muttered.

"Indeed," agreed Archie. "Nonetheless, useful in their place. As we can attest to on an occasion such as this."

The horse pulled us out of the dark countryside and towards the edges of a town, where house windows cast rectangles of light.

"To where shall I take you, my dear *Maggie?*" asked Archie.

"Nowhere," I mumbled. "I have nowhere to go."

"But this is terrible, disgraceful!" Archie cried in distress. He jerked on the reins in his nervous anxiety and the horse threw up its head and snorted. "You are heartsick!" Archie said. "And alone in the world! This is not right, *Maggie* of St. Ives. I must find succor for you."

He negotiated several more streets in tense silence. When I peered sideways at him through my burning eyelids, I saw his pale face arranged in a pattern of frowning concentration. He kept playing with the reins, and the horse kept snorting. I could see why Archie and horses did not get along — there was too much passion in Archie. He unsettled the animals.

"I will deliver you to Hazelbrae House," he announced suddenly. "The Society is a family to the friendless, an open door to the needy."

"The Barnardo Society?" I asked.

"Indeed," agreed Archie. "Indeed, where else should I

take a Celtic queen who has lost her way so far from the sound of the sea?" And he rattled the whip nervously in its socket, so that the horse plunged around the next corner much too fast, and the buggy wheels almost scraped a lamppost. Archie appeared not to notice.

Suddenly, we were outside a huge house full of windows, and Archie was lifting me carefully down from the buggy and leading me up a path. Bushes and pine trees sighed in the warm, gusty wind. The house loomed above us. We climbed the verandah steps and Archie knocked peremptorily on the door with the knob of his cane. When the door opened, he bowed from the waist as well as he could with me leaning against him.

"Dear madam," he said to the woman silhouetted against the light, "behold, a child in need of your open door. Maggie is an orphan, whom I met on the road. I beg of you, assist her in her time of crisis."

I swayed forward and the woman let out a strange exclamation of surprise, then everything began to spin: the woman's white starched apron, the walls, Archie's anxious green eyes. "Catch her," I heard the woman say, from far away, then everything went black.

◇ ◇

After years had gone by — that's how it felt to me — I came half awake in a bed with gray blankets. I stared at the pale walls and the morning light, I heard my blood thudding in my ears, I felt my skin burning. Then I sank back into blackness. The next time I awoke, the light had changed position on the walls. I'm in Hazelbrae House, in Peterborough, I thought. I'm back where I started from six years ago, before I ever went to the Howards' farm. Will they send me back there again? Will Mr. Walker, the stiff home visitor, walk through the door and tell me I'm an ungrateful child?

I struggled to sit up but I felt too weak, and my skin was still burning. My mouth was dry, and I wondered where my jar of water was. But it was empty, I reminded myself. Maybe someone could bring me water. I wanted to call, but I didn't know what name to use. I fell asleep trying to remember the names of the ladies who had worked at Hazelbrae six years before.

Next time, I awoke to voices. I turned my head on the pillow and stared at the room's closed door.

". . . sleeping. But I thought you should examine her just to be sure," said a woman.

"Yes, of course. Who brought her here?" asked a man with a deep, firm voice.

"Mr. Archer, that mad Englishman. He paints, I believe."

"Ah, yes. Him. Well, he has a good heart whatever else may be said of him. Where did he find the girl?"

"Beside the road a mile east of town. She was sitting in the wet grass, almost fainting."

"Thank you, Miss Miller. I'll examine her now," the man's voice said, and the door swung open into my room.

The man's legs, in brown flannel, came towards my bed and behind them I glimpsed the woman's starched apron. Then the man bent gravely over me, with his woolly brown beard and his kind, patient eyes. "I am

Dr. Fisher," he explained, "and I'm here to see how you are. Do you know where you are?"

"Where all the orphans go," I said bitterly. "I'm in Hazelbrae House."

He grasped my wrist in his warm, firm fingers and counted my pulse while staring at the watch he had pulled from his waistcoat pocket. The watch's gold chain swung to and fro as he counted. Then he opened his soft, brown leather bag, pulled out a thermometer and slipped it cold and hard beneath my tongue. He held it up to the window light afterwards, and tutted. "You have a fever, Maggie," he said. "You must rest and regain your strength. Miss Miller tells me you were walking. Had you come far?"

"From Bridgenorth to Keene and back again up Settler's Line," I said stiffly. "I went to find my twin sister but she was gone. They sent her back again."

"Ahhh," the doctor said, a long sound sliding out of his mouth as if he suddenly understood something. "You have had a great shock, Maggie, but I think all will come well again. You must rest some more first. Miss Miller will bring you a drink."

He straightened his long legs, and moved towards the rustling apron. "I will prescribe something for the fever," he said to the woman. "No more excitement just yet. Rest is the best cure. Exhaustion and dehydration are what ails her."

The door closed behind them both. Although there was silence in my room, I could hear muffled noises from other rooms; children's voices, once some singing, dishes clattering in a kitchen. I remembered what it had been like living here before; the jostle of orphans like me, the cots squeezed together in the bedrooms, the chores we did each day. My life has come right around in a circle, I thought dismally.

Then the door opened and Miss Miller's starched apron rustled over to my bed. "Drink this, now, Maggie," she said firmly and held a glass to my mouth as I sat up. The liquid was bitter and I wrinkled my nose and gulped it down fast. "Rest now," she said, and rustled away again.

The next time I woke, the light had moved back to its morning position on the ceiling. Had I slept for a whole afternoon and a night? I stretched my legs out long and thin between the sheets. They felt rested and strong, but I remembered that I didn't have to do any more walking. My skin was cool and my head felt steady. I lay and listened to the sounds in the house for a while. Then I wondered which room they had put me in, and I turned on my side to look at it.

On the floor by my bed was a small, oval rug woven from rags. I followed one piece of rag with my eyes, a yellow one, the color of marigolds, and noticed how it was woven in and out around the other, duller pieces of cloth. Across from my bed was a chest of drawers, with an oval mirror reflecting light from the window. I counted the six glass knobs on the drawers. The edge of a piece of fabric, something white, was caught in one of the drawers. I wondered if I should get out of bed. I glanced at the mirror, to see if I could see myself in its oval world.

There *was* a reflection of a girl there — but it wasn't me. It was of someone sitting by the window, on a chair with a high, straight back. Morning sunlight burned in her red hair where it tumbled over her shoulders. Her freckles were pale yellow, like sand. Her blue eyes stared out at the lilac trees and the meadow. She was a girl inside a bubble of glass, a looking-glass world, a dream.

"Thomasina?" I whispered.

CHAPTER
FOURTEEN

"Maggie?" the girl in the window said softly.

Our names hung in the space between us. Goose-bumps ran up my arms and down my spine. I stared, fascinated, as she stood up slowly. It was like watching myself, it was like seeing a reflection come to life and step out of the glass into my world. She was thin and tall, with a bandage wrapped around her right ankle, and she walked to my bed with a limp. Her pale, blue cotton dress fanned over the gray blanket as she sat down. I could hardly believe she was there; I was afraid to even touch her. We just stared and stared at one another.

"What are you doing here?" I finally asked, in a whisper.

"We don't have to whisper," she whispered back. Suddenly we both began to laugh, the noise catching in our throats, our eyes filling up and running over, our stomachs hurting.

"What are you doing here?" I gasped. "They said they sent you back, I thought you had gone back to England."

"Who said?" she asked. When she spoke, I noticed

that her teeth were straighter than mine. Mine had little gaps between them, but hers were even.

"The woman at the farm, at the Smiths' farm at Keene."

"Were you there?" she asked in surprise.

"The Barnardo visitor said you were there, so I walked over to find you. But the woman was horrible!"

"That was Mrs. Smith. I fell off the wagon at barley harvest time and I thought my ankle was broken. They bandaged it up and then they were mad at me because I couldn't work. I had to hobble around indoors and do housework. And then I had to do outside chores, but I was still hobbling, and they got even madder and sent me back here."

I could feel hair prickling on top of my head. "When we had barley harvest at our farm," I told her, "I fell over one day with a hurt ankle — my right ankle. But there wasn't anything wrong with it. It just hurt inside, throbbed. The hired man said I'd sprained it, but it started to hurt *before* I fell over."

Thomasina's face stretched into an amazed stillness. "Do you think —"

"It was the same day," I agreed. "It was when you fell off the wagon. What else? It was your pain I felt in my ankle. And you know how you came to Canada in the spring? I started dreaming about you in the spring, in April."

"I've been dreaming about you, too," she said solemnly. She was almost whispering again. Our hands reached out and clasped; our thin, hard fingers locked together as if they would never let go. Our white knuckles made rows of bumps, like camels' backs. We hugged each other fiercely; we pressed our freckles together. Her red, loose hair hung on both our shoulders. I buried my face in it; it felt like home, like home after a long, long journey.

"What are *you* doing here?" she asked at last, and we loosened our grip on one another and sat back.

I told her about running away from the Howards', about Archie and the gypsies, how Alice took Kathleen and Lizzy to the city. I told her about my garden, about pigs and cows, winter mornings when the pump handle would freeze your bare fingers, and summer nights when the house was hot enough to melt candle wax. I described the beautiful, forbidden lake and the frightening fire at the neighbors' cabin. Six years of my life came tumbling out, all jumbled up but finally getting to the place they belonged. I knew that Thomasina was saving every word.

Then she told me about Nancledra, about looking after the old aunt who was an invalid, and about going to school with farm children instead of fishermen's children. I saved all her words too — the ones about making blackberry jam, and singing in chapel, and making friends with a miner's son.

"But what happened?" I asked. "Why aren't you still there?"

"Aunt got pneumonia and died, and the house was rented out to some other people. They buried her in Zennor churchtown; the miners carried her coffin all the way over the fields because she wanted to lie by her husband. Then some neighbors put me on the train to a place called Basingstoke, and the Barnardo people met me at the station. That was last autumn. I spent months there, with the other girls. Then in the spring, when the ships could sail, I came to Canada."

"Were you seasick?"

"No," she said scornfully. "But it was miserable, windy and cold. And in the fog we saw icebergs bigger than huge houses, all white and blue!"

"Let's see how much you've grown then," I said, pushing back the blankets and climbing out of bed. "Turn your back."

She remembered what to do. It was what our father made us do when he came home from sea — to tease us, to see if we had grown bigger in a few days. He always stood us back to back, bony shoulder blade to shoulder blade. Now we did it again, one more time, far from home.

"I'm still a little taller than you," I said. *You'm growin' like young Turks*, my father's voice said in my head. I wondered if Thomasina could hear it in her own head. "Do you remember?" I asked her.

"You'm growin' like young Turks," she said, mimicking my father's voice.

The goosebumps ran down my spine again. "Oh, I can't believe it!" I cried. "I can't believe you're real and you're here! It's like — like going back in time!"

But it was more than that. It was like finding myself again, the Maggie Curnow who'd got lost six years ago, when the Howards' wagon hauled me out into the dark countryside of a strange land.

We laid our flat, warm palms together and compared our fingers, the shape of our thumbs. Our fingernails each had a little pale shape, like a moon, at the bottom. My nails were edged with dirt, but Thomasina's were clean. We sat on the floor and laid our feet sole to sole and saw that my feet were slightly longer — but our toes were the same shape.

"Is your ankle broken?" I asked, but Thomasina shook her head.

"Dr. Fisher looked at it when I came here, and he said it's a bad sprain but it will heal."

I picked my flour bag up from the table by the bed, where someone had placed it, and tipped the three shells into my hand. "Remember these?"

Thomasina stared and nodded. "I gave them to you the day we left St. Ives," she said wonderingly. "You kept them, all these years." She touched the shells carefully with the tip of one finger, as if they were very fragile and precious.

The door swung open and tall Miss Miller came in, smiling. "Like two roses off the same bush," she said. "And it looks as though Maggie is feeling better." She laid her hand flat on my forehead, feeling my temperature. "Dr. Fisher says if you're cool and feeling stronger, you may get up," she continued. "Why don't the two of you go out for some air in the garden? You can be excused from your duties for the rest of this morning, Thomasina, being as how it's so long since you've seen your sister."

Thomasina's face glowed. "Thank you, Miss," she said.

"Maggie, these are your clothes. The girls washed them for you." Miss Miller deposited my limp dress onto the end of the bed and then left us again.

Thomasina fetched me water in a china pitcher decorated with pink roses, and I washed my face, then combed out my hair. It was much longer than Thomasina's but the exact same color. When I had braided it again, I wrapped the braids around my head the way that I always did, and pinned them in place while Thomasina watched. It was funny to think that she had never seen me do this. There were ways in which we didn't know each other anymore.

Outside, we strolled arm in arm around the meadow, sometimes talking and sometimes being silent, listening to our feet swooshing through the grass. It was hard not to stare at Thomasina all the time. Everything about her — every tiny detail — fascinated me. Squinting sideways, I looked at her golden eyelashes, the glints of gold in her red hair, the crisp fold in the green ribbon tying that hair back, the way she walked with a bobbing gait. I noticed how her thin wrists were, no bigger around than my own, and how she smiled with her lips closed, the way our mother used to.

"What work do you do here?" I asked.

"I'm doing secretarial work for Miss Miller, who's the matron. There's another secretary too, and we write letters and run errands in town and open the door for callers."

"Do you like it?" I asked curiously.

"Oh, it's much better than the farm! Miss Miller is fair and kind, and the work is easy. There are always people to talk to and Miss Taylor, the other secretary, is nice."

"Do you like being inside all day?"

"I don't mind it. I hated the farm, it was so hard and lonely, the people were horrible and I didn't know how to do anything."

"You were always happier inside than me," I said.

"Was I? What else do you remember?"

"I remember . . . how you could never eat a whole pasty. You used to always save a piece of one end, and put it in your pocket to eat later."

"But it always got sat on and smushed up."

Laughter ripped out of us, climbing on the sunny air. Pine trees sighed overhead, soft as waves on a distant beach. Over on the porch of Hazelbrae House, two girls were winding a ball of wool. They turned their faces towards us when we laughed. I could feel pain trickling out of me like water, leaving me empty and light and warm as sunshine.

"What else do you remember?" Thomasina asked.

"I remember . . . you used to sneak milk and put it outside for a gray cat and you named him Ashes. When father came home from having a pint at The Sloop he used to trip over him and call him a bleddy heathen!"

We were laughing again, hurting our stomachs, creasing up our wet eyes.

"And I remember you jabbing cousins with your sharp elbows, Maggie, when they called you Magpie."

"Yes, after Mother died," I agreed and we fell silent,

and listened to the grass against our feet again.

"Greetings, fair ladies!" called a voice, and there was Archie's familiar figure, leaping nimbly from his penny-farthing on the road outside the fence. He lifted his straw boater as I waved, and swung it through the air.

"Who is he?" Thomasina asked, and I took her hand and towed her towards the fence where she gazed at Archie shyly.

"This is my very good friend, Mr. Archer," I said solemnly, because at that moment I knew that I might never have found Thomasina if Archie hadn't rescued me and brought me to Hazelbrae in a rented buggy.

"Enchanted," murmured Archie. "Enchanted to meet you, Miss Thomasina. I called by to ascertain whether all was well with Miss Maggie, but I can see that she is fully recovered from her arduous journey. And now, my greatest pleasure would be to paint you together, two Celtic beauties in a garden."

"You'll have to ask Matron," I said.

"Indeed, and so I shall very soon," agreed Archie. "It would be an honor." With another flourish of his hat, he mounted his penny-farthing, executed a circle in the road, and wobbled away.

As we leaned on the fence and watched, Matron called to us from the verandah. "Tea time," Thomasina explained to me, and we trailed back towards the house. My body felt weak and dragging, as though all its different parts were coming adrift from one another. My stomach growled uneasily.

The dining room was filled with a babble of voices

and the harsh scraping of boots but as Thomasina and I entered, silence fell. Rows of faces turned towards us, heads swiveled, eyes studied us. Then an excited murmuring broke out.

"Cor blimey, look at them!" "Twins!" "How you know which one is which?" "Cor! Fancy lookin' so alike!"

Thomasina gripped my hand and tugged me towards an empty place on one side of a long table. "Just ignore them," she whispered, and I followed her with my head high, while all the other children's heads swiveled to catch our every move.

"Silence for grace!" Matron said firmly, and all the heads bowed and the eyelashes flickered shut. Under the table, my knee pressed against Thomasina's knee and my bony elbow nudged hers. While Matron said grace, I could feel my heart swelling up, growing bigger and stronger, making room for love again after so many years.

❖ ❖

It was easy to fit back into the routines of Hazelbrae House. I remembered the prayers after a breakfast of oatmeal and cocoa, how we all stood packed together in the kitchen while Matron droned on about our blessings. I remembered the sweeping central staircase and how it felt to polish the wooden spindles with a soft cloth. Every morning, I scrubbed tabletops and washed floors and sorted laundry with other girls, whom I mostly ignored. I only wanted to be with Thomasina; all my thoughts and energy were wrapped up in thinking about her. I found reasons to linger in the hallway, outside the office door, and to catch glimpses of her red head bent over a desk as she wrote letters for Miss Miller. Sometimes, when I was scrubbing a floor, she would walk past, and every time I saw her coming my heart gave a leap of shock and love. Every time, it was like seeing myself, watching myself cross a room. I couldn't get used to it.

All morning, while we worked, the house smelled of lye and polish, and of the soup cooking for our lunch. We were supervised by two lady staff: dumpy, gray Miss Fitzgerald, and skinny, young Miss Weaver. *Don't waste the polish*, *get a dry cloth*, *scrub harder than that*, *mind your own business*, *idle hands do the devil's work*, *finish this job first* their voices told us hour after hour. Thomasina and I sat together for every lunch, leaning over the steam of our vegetable broth and smiling at each other with the corners of our eyes.

At night we slept in the long upper room, crowded with cots. I remembered the smooth pillows and scratchy gray blankets, the whispers in the dark, the muffled sobs. Sometimes, in those first nights back at Hazelbrae, I would wake up and listen to the hushed breathing of Thomasina in the cot next to mine. Each time, a cool thrill of disbelief and joy tingled over my skin. I would reach out an arm and touch her lightly, feeling her warmth and her tough bones. I could hardly believe, still, that she was really here and that we were together again.

Sometimes, after lunch, Miss Miller would give Thomasina and me permission to take the small children out into the meadow and let them play. We sat in the grass, with our arms wrapped around our legs, while the children chased each other in games of tag or crouched behind bushes for hide and seek. One afternoon, while we were outside, a buggy arrived at the house and a man and woman climbed from it.

"They're coming to find a child," Thomasina guessed, and she was right.

After some time had passed, the man and woman reappeared with a tall, skinny boy beside them. The boy moved with a nervous, jerky walk, like a puppet being pulled on invisible strings. The man carried the boy's trunk; it was like the one I had left behind on the Howards' farm and might never see again. The man lifted the trunk into the buggy, the boy lunged in beside it, then the man and woman climbed up and they all drove away.

"I wonder where they're going," I said, and I wondered about the boy too: if he would be given a papered room on the top floor of a farmhouse, or if he would have to sleep over the woodshed in a cramped space. I knew without thinking about it what his days would be like: the black, early mornings when he called the cows across the fields, the burning afternoons when he bent to his work, the long rows of turnips and corn he would hoe. Would they beat him with a belt? Would he be teased at school and called a Home child? I shivered and Thomasina glanced sympathetically at me.

"Don't fret," she said. "You won't be sent to the Howards'. There was another girl who ran away and came here, and Miss Miller didn't make her go back to the farm she had escaped from."

"Where did she go then?"

"To a lady in town who wanted a domestic."

"They might send me away again to a different farm," I said sadly. "We might not see each other much."

"We won't let them do that," Thomasina shot back quickly, her face suddenly pale and her freckles standing out. She stuck her chin in the air, and I remembered that she had always done this when her mind was made up about something. Maybe I did it too.

"What about you? What will happen to you?" I asked, twisting grass stems around my fingers.

"Miss Miller says I can live here at Hazelbrae and be her secretary. She won't send me away, and I can earn wages and have them saved for me until I'm twenty-one."

"Is that what you want to do?"

"Yes," she replied.

"I would like to stay here in town too," I said thoughtfully. "Maybe Miss Miller can find me a house to work in nearby, so that we could still see each other."

The thought of being separated from Thomasina filled my stomach with an anxious cramp. Surely Miss Miller would not be mean enough to send me away into the countryside, away to another farm at the end of many miles of dusty roads and silence.

"If she tries to separate us, I shall run away again," I vowed fiercely.

"But then you couldn't come here and visit me," Thomasina pointed out.

"We can both run away," I said.

We stared at each other in the hot sunshine, while the children's high-pitched calls echoed around us like bird song.

"Where would we go?" Thomasina asked, and I shrugged.

"Toronto, maybe?" I said, but I could feel that I didn't want to do this. I knew what it was like to be lost and hungry on a nameless road. Another time, there might not be a kind stranger like Archie to rescue me.

"We'll just have to wait and see what happens," Thomasina said, and I nodded unwillingly.

After that afternoon, I began worrying. At night, lying in a darkness full of whispering breaths, and with the scratchy blanket draped over my legs, I worried about being separated from Thomasina again. I worried about a buggy driving up one day and strangers asking for me, about Matron packing another trunk for me, about Thomasina standing on the verandah and waving goodbye. Every time I got this picture in my mind, my heart thumped so loud in my chest, that I thought it would wake the other children. But only Thomasina awoke, and reached out her long arm in the darkness, and gripped my hand until I fell asleep again.

CHAPTER
FIFTEEN

One misty morning in early September, when the grass was drenched with dew and the trees hung still, Matron said that she had an announcement to make. All around me in the kitchen, children fidgeted and murmured. Thomasina's arm was pressed against mine. I had been staring out past Matron's shoulder into the warm, damp garden, but when she mentioned an announcement, my eyes fastened themselves on her face and a quiver of fear passed through me. What if she was sending me away; what if she was announcing where I was going? But that was silly, she wouldn't do that in front of everybody, would she? Thomasina and I shot each other a puzzled glance.

"As you know," Matron began, "this house was generously donated to the Barnardo Society so that you would all have a warm, safe home in which to stay in this new land. Many, many children have passed through this house and gone on to become successful citizens of this country."

Thomasina and I glanced at each other again, rolling our eyes, but around me the smaller children were staring solemnly at Matron with their eyes wide open.

"It takes a great deal of money to look after all you children, to buy the food you eat, the clothes you wear. Other people's hard work is what takes care of each one of you. And now, to raise more money, the good people of this city of Peterborough have agreed to come and join us for a harvest tea. We will provide the tea, and people will pay admission to come. We will all have to help to make the tea a success . . ."

Matron's voice droned on, but I began to watch a chickadee in a branch of the forsythia bush outside the window. I knew that Miss Weaver and Miss Fitzgerald would make sure that we knew all about the extra work needed to make ready for this tea. Around me, children shifted and fidgeted until at last Matron dismissed everyone. "You may all go to your tasks, except for Thomasina and Maggie," she finished, and another quiver of fear passed through me. Maybe she was going to tell me to say goodbye to Thomasina; tell me to pack, to prepare to drive away in a buggy to some place I had never been before.

When the room was empty, she smiled at us. "Girls, your help will be needed more than ever in the next week," she said. "Nevertheless, I have agreed with Mr. Archer, the painter, that you may pose for him in the garden. The picture will be raffled at the tea. That is all for now."

I breathed a sigh of relief, and I heard Thomasina's breath sigh out of her too. We were safe for another day, or another week. Safe until the harvest tea, I thought, because Miss Miller had said my help would be needed.

I had been right about Miss Weaver and Miss Fitzgerald making sure that we knew what extra tasks to do. All day long they chivvied and organized us, set us to sweeping and polishing, to beating rugs outside on the clothesline, to darning socks and mending sheets and polishing floors until we could see our reflections in them. They were determined to make the house "a credit to dear Dr. Barnardo, who made this all possible." I wished that the great man would come and do the work himself, and impress the good people of the city with what Miss Weaver called "his grand vision." Then *we* wouldn't have to worry about impressing them with our spotless dresses and tidy hair, our perfectly risen scones and our perfectly mixed cakes.

All day long, fruity steam poured from the kitchen where a team of girls was making apple jelly. In the laundry, the smell of soap drifted over the heads of another group, busy pummeling sheets and hose and aprons with red, wrinkled hands. Even Thomasina was requested to leave her office duties, and she and I were sent onto the verandah to darn socks.

It was peaceful out there. Some of the bushes were beginning to turn color, their leaves growing thin and translucent and pink. The sunshine was low and soft, not the burning glare of summer, but the mellow light of autumn. Soon the nights would grow longer and colder;

soon summer would be over. Small birds chattered on the fence, fluttering in excitement.

"They're planning their journey south," I said to Thomasina. It was hard to imagine how distant they would be by winter, how far they would take their tiny bodies in search of warmth and safety. I wondered where *I* would be then, if *I* would be far away, if *I* would be safe and warm. Anxiety gnawed at me.

"Tell me about your friends," Thomasina said, as she picked another sock from the basket between us, and deftly threaded her needle.

"I have a friend right here in town," I said a little shyly. "He's called Harold and he works for a furniture maker."

"Can I meet him?"

"Maybe sometime," I said, but suddenly I didn't want Thomasina to meet Harold. When he saw how much alike we were, he might not be able to tell us apart. I might not be special to him anymore, just one half of a pair. And even Archie, if he came to paint us, might not know which girl he had shared his lunch with on the road. I squirmed uneasily in my chair. I wasn't used to being with Thomasina; I wasn't sure anymore that I wanted us to be so much the same. I was used to being alone, and unique, and the only girl with red hair.

I sneaked a look at Thomasina. I was half afraid she might be reading my thoughts. But her eyes were cast down, and her hands were busy making tight, neat stitches.

"Tell me more about Mae Beth. Will I ever meet her?" she asked.

"I don't know. She doesn't live in town," I replied, and

suddenly I missed Mae Beth, with her yellow curls and her flouncing skirts. I wondered if she would like Thomasina just as much as she liked me. I could see that being a twin might mean I had to share everything: my face, my name, my friends.

"Do you think I'll make any friends here?" Thomasina asked wistfully, and I stared at her in surprise. "I mean, real friends," she said. "Not orphans living here for a little while and then moving away to other places where I never see them again."

"I don't know," I replied. "Just be glad *you* don't have to move away. You get to stay behind and be taken care of, just like last time."

"What last time?" she asked.

There was a sudden stillness between us. I could feel words bunching up in my mouth, hot and hard and mean. Out of the corner of my eye, I saw the little birds swoop away in a rush, as though something had frightened them. From inside Hazelbrae, the sounds of voices and clattering dishes came faintly.

"What last time?" Thomasina repeated, and I opened my mouth and let the stony words fly out at her, hitting her wide blue eyes and her freckled cheeks and her long, pale limbs.

"Last time, when I got sent away from Uncle Jan's house," I said angrily. "When you hid upstairs while they put me into the pony trap. Did you know what they were doing with me? Did you know you were being kept and I wasn't?"

My hands jerked in my lap, stabbing my needle into

my thumb. "Damn!" I swore, the way Willy did when Tom told him what to do. I dropped the needle onto the floor, and glared at Thomasina as if I hated her.

I did hate her. Right then, I did. All the anger that had kept me going, had kept me strong and proud when Willy teased me, when the cows ignored my calls, when Lizzy fussed at me — all that anger came boiling to the surface of my mind.

"You got to stay with a nice old aunt! I got sent away! I cried all the way to London," I hissed. "I bet you didn't even care. You were safe, you were loved. You needn't think you are any better than me, just because they kept you."

"I don't think —" Thomasina started, but I interrupted her.

"I've got along just fine all these years. I learned everything I had to learn on the farm. But it wasn't easy. It was hard! It was hard being so far from home and being sent away by my own family and being teased and being cold at night and working in the fields and in the house —"

I stopped to catch my breath. I was panting with anger.

"I guess you think you're better than me, but you can't milk a cow or stook grain. You can't even help harvest barley without falling off the wagon!"

I had gone too far. My mouth was empty and cold. I pressed my lips together hard, in a straight line, and stared at the needle lying on the floor. Thomasina had tears in her eyes, and I wouldn't look at her, I wouldn't reach my hand out to where her hands lay open and still in her lap. I thought of how she reached her hand out to me at night, when I lay worrying in my cot, but I pushed the thought away. She deserved to cry now. Her life had been easy and happy all the years that mine was hard and lonely.

She stood up, and her needle fell onto the floor beside mine. Then the sock she had been working on landed on top of it with a soft plop. I heard her feet move away across the verandah. The screen door squeaked, then swung shut with a thump.

I lifted my eyes from the sock basket and I was alone. I sat there for a long time, numb and frozen and stiff, until Miss Weaver came bustling out and told me that she needed help turning mattresses.

"Gracious sakes! Is that all the mending you got done?" she asked sharply, staring at the one sock I had darned. She snatched up the basket of other, unmended socks and told me, "Hurry up — and wipe that sulky look off your face while you're at it."

That night, Thomasina and I climbed into bed without looking at each other, without speaking. She didn't reach out her arm to me in the darkness. Hour after hour, while the moon rose behind the pine trees in the meadow, I lay on my back and stared into the darkness. Pain filled me up, pouring into the hole where my anger had been before I shaped it into the words I threw at Thomasina. There's something wrong with me, I thought. I'm a wicked person. I'm like Willy.

I remembered how angry I had been when Willy

spoiled my flowers, and how I had blamed my anger on him. I had a right to be angry, because he had done me wrong. And Thomasina's done me wrong too, my thoughts cried in the night. She let me be sent away. She could have broken free of Aunt's hold and run after me. She could have followed me to London. But part of me knew that this wasn't true, that Aunt had been too strong and Thomasina had been too young.

I hate her because she's had life easy, I thought. I hate her because she hasn't had to suffer like I have. Here she is at Hazelbrae, all warm and safe, and she didn't have to live even one winter on the Smiths' farm. And all the years I was working at the Howards', she was taken care of by Father's old aunt. She was getting my share of love. That's why there was no love for me.

But then I remembered how we had clung together when we met, how I had buried my face in her hair and how it had been like coming home. I remembered how she smiled the way our mother used to, and how she could mimic our father's voice. How could I hate the other half of myself?

I remembered how once, when my father had left some fishing net twine in a ball, Ashes the cat had played with it. He had got the twine all tangled and snarled, so that father couldn't even find the beginning or the end of it. That was what my thoughts were like, as I lay rigid in my cot. My thoughts were knotted and snarled up and tangled, all leading nowhere, going around in circles.

I wondered if Thomasina was asleep. A child coughed at the other end of the room, and closer to me another child was snoring. I sat up and leaned my back against the tepid wall, and watched the moonlight move across the curtains. Tomorrow Archie was coming to paint our pictures and I was going to be exhausted and sullen. I wasn't going to enjoy it at all. And Thomasina would be miserable too, I thought. It would be my fault.

I remembered Archie telling me that I had flowers in my heart. He was wrong. What I had in my heart was hard, rocky lumps of anger. Then I remembered what Miss Hooper, my old teacher, had said about flowers being objects of beauty, and how a thing of beauty was a joy forever. But now, I thought, I'm a person just like Willy. I go around spoiling things the way he spoiled my beautiful flowers. I've spoiled Thomasina's happiness and I've spoiled our friendship.

Shame seeped through me, thin and cold. My skin crawled. I can't blame what has happened on the farm, I thought. I don't live at the farm anymore. If I am going to leave the farm behind, I have to stop carrying all these mean feelings in my heart.

I have to tell Thomasina that I'm sorry. I have to decide to be a person with a heart like a garden.

I slid down the wall, and Thomasina opened her eyes. I saw them glint in the moonlight. I stretched my arm out, but she didn't take my hand. She closed her eyes and turned on her other side and a great wave of loneliness broke over me, cold as sea water. I would have to wait for morning to set things right.

In the morning, Thomasina and I dressed silently in the narrow space between our cots. We were careful not to touch each other, not to bump into one another. Whenever I glanced at her, she was looking somewhere else. My stomach was so cold and heavy that I could barely stand up straight. Miserably, I followed the stream of children down to breakfast, and, miserably, I spooned oatmeal into my mouth. I could barely swallow.

"Hurry up, Maggie. There's work to be done," scolded Miss Weaver, but I still couldn't swallow properly.

Finally the bowls were all collected, the children dispersed, and Miss Weaver sent Thomasina and me back outside to darn socks.

"They're to be all darned by lunchtime, or you can work through lunch," she said crossly to my bent shoulders as I opened the screen door. Thomasina sat silently beside me, and we reached into the sock basket and threaded our needles.

Silence pressed down on me, filled my mouth, closed my throat. I had to speak. I cleared my throat but Thomasina didn't look up from her work.

"Thomasina, I'm sorry," I said at last. "I'm really, truly sorry."

Still, there was silence. At last she let out a long sigh and looked at me. Her eyes were fierce.

"You've got everything wrong, all wrong," she said.

"What do you mean?"

"They didn't keep me because they loved me better."

"Why then?" I asked.

"Listen," she said. "Just be quiet and listen. It was Aunt Queenie who made all the arrangements. She wanted us both to go to Nancledra, to father's Aunt Mabel. But

Aunt Mabel wasn't strong and she said she could only take one child. So then Aunt Queenie arranged for one child to go to the Barnardo people in London."

Thomasina paused and I gulped noisily. Every nerve in my body was stretched tight, wanting to know what she would say next, how she would explain what had happened.

"So," she continued, "Aunt Queenie made the arrangement for one child to go with the minister's wife to London, and the other to go to Aunt Mabel's place. It didn't matter which child went where. She never decided which of us to send away to Canada. She never told Aunt Mabel who would go to Nancledra. She just grabbed the first child who came down the stairs that morning, and she put that child in the first pony trap to arrive at the door. You were the first child down, Maggie. And the minister's wife was waiting at the door. So you got sent to London. That's all."

She tied a knot in the end of a piece of wool, and snipped it clean with a little pair of silver scissors.

"How do you know all this?" I asked.

"Because when I came downstairs, you were already leaving. And afterwards Uncle Jan came in the back door and asked Aunt Queenie what was going on. So she told him, and he ran to the station to bring you home again. He said you'd be sent away to Canada over his dead body. He said they would keep you there with them."

"He came to the station, running," I whispered, "but he was too late to catch me. The train was moving."

"So I know what happened because, when Uncle Jan

got home again from the station, he asked Aunt Queenie how she'd decided which child to send. And she said she didn't decide, she just grabbed the first child down the stairs."

I took a deep breath. I could hardly believe my ears. All these years, I had been angry about something that hadn't even happened. I had been miserable because they hadn't loved me, but I had been wrong. Thomasina could have been sent just as easily as I had been. It had all been chance.

"And something else," Thomasina said. "When Uncle Jan heard about this, he was so angry at Aunt Queenie, that he broke her best oven dish. And he yelled at her like he'd gone mad. He said what a beautiful maid you were, Maggie, and how you were spunky like your mother and how he wished he could have gone to Canada himself to save you from being sent away."

"Really?" I asked. I tried to imagine my aunt's cramped, dingy kitchen and my wild cousins, all standing staring while my gentle uncle yelled and broke things — because of me! Because he loved me and wanted to keep me there in his home!

"And it wasn't like you think at Nancledra either," said Thomasina. "Aunt Mabel wasn't a kind old lady who looked after me. She was a tartar. She had hairs on her chin, and she fussed about everything, and I slept in a tiny, cold room at the back of the house, where the walls grew mold and the wind cried under the eaves. It wasn't cozy or easy, Maggie."

"I'm sorry," I mumbled. I could hardly believe how

wrong I had been all these years; how angry I had been about nothing. "I didn't know," I said. "I'm sorry, Thomasina."

"It's all right now," she said, and our hands stretched out and clasped tightly, our knuckles pointed as camels' humps, our blue eyes smiling.

I kept smiling all morning, while we darned socks as fast as we could. We didn't want to miss lunch. Over and over I played the pictures through my head: Uncle Jan trying to bring me home from the station, Thomasina fetching and carrying for a cross old woman with a hairy chin. I felt as if all the hard rocks in me were dissolving, turning into soap bubbles, floating away. I felt empty and light and clean.

When Archie arrived just before lunch, I ran across the grass to meet him, feeling as if I was skimming, almost flying. His green eyes twinkled at me. After he had eaten lunch with Miss Miller, he set up an easel in the shade of a pine tree, and Thomasina and I sat in the dappled sunlight nearby and arranged flowers in vases. This was partly because they were needed to decorate tables at the harvest tea, and partly because Archie wanted us looking "charming."

When he sketched us, his eyes stopped twinkling and got still and focused and intense, like the eyes of a cat when it's hunting. I felt as if his eyes were taking in our every detail, and I knew then that he would never get muddled up about which girl he had shared his lunch with along the side of the road. I was right, too. When he spoke over the top of his easel, he always called me

Maggie, and he always called Thomasina by her own name. I needn't have worried about losing my friends; I was still myself.

While Archie worked, the sunlight slipped across the grass, and across the skirts of our best dresses. Every time that I caught Thomasina's eye, I smiled. I felt as if her words had set me free.

There was nothing left to worry about except where I would be sent.

CHAPTER SIXTEEN

"Spread these over the tables, Maggie," Miss Weaver said, handing me a heavy pile of folded white tablecloths.

I carried them outside into the sunshine, where the boys were setting up trestle tables on the grass. Behind me followed a procession of other girls, with vases of flowers, cutlery, trays of scones and fruitcake, jars of jelly, paper napkins and lace doilies, teacups and sugar bowls. The boys were shouting and whistling as they worked, and the girls chattered and laughed. Excitement filled the air because today was the harvest tea, and all our routines were being turned upside down. Soon our meadow would fill with visitors, picnic rugs, and unknown voices.

I began to unfold the tablecloths, shaking them out wildly against the blue sky, their snowy folds billowing like sails. Thomasina appeared beside me and, taking one end of each cloth, she helped me cover the tables. We spread the cloths flat, smoothing wrinkles away with the palms of our hands. Beside us, a girl dropped a plate of scones; the browned buns lay scattered in the grass.

With a shriek, she bent to pick them up, and the rest of us huddled around her, laughing as we hid her from Miss Weaver's sharp eyes.

"Here she comes," someone hissed, and the girl blew grass off the last bun and set it back on the plate beside the others.

"Now then, girls, on with your work," Miss Weaver said sharply. Her eyes swiveled suspiciously from face to face, but only our smothered laughter gave us away and she couldn't decide what we had been doing. "Back to the kitchen for more trays," she commanded. "Thomasina, you fetch the raffle tickets for Mr. Archer's painting. Maggie, help Miss McPherson with her flowers."

I turned to look in the direction in which Miss Weaver was pointing, and I saw a short woman coming through the front gate of Hazelbrae House.

Afternoon sun streamed around her shoulders, and made a circle of light behind her head. In the bushel basket she carried on one hip, flowers glowed like pieces of colored glass in a church window. Her whole basket blazed with a golden light. I stood and stared, and then I began to run forward to meet her. I wanted to be part of the picture, to bury my hands in her glowing flowers, her basket of light.

"Now then, are ye coming to help me with these?" the woman asked when I reached her. She gave the basket on her hip a sideways nod, and I looked for the first time at her face. Her skin was soft and lined with age, but her cheeks were pink and, under thick, white hair, her eyes were bright and curious. She was dressed all in blue: a blue and white striped muslin dress, a white lace collar pinned at the throat with a blue cameo brooch, a blue shawl with a long fringe.

"I'm Miss McPherson," she said. Her voice was firm and warm, and her letters were blurred by a Scottish accent.

"I'm Maggie — and I love flowers!" I blurted out, and bending down I buried my face in her basket, the petals fluttering against my cheeks, my mind filled with fragments of golden light.

"Well, ye're the right girl to help me then," Miss McPherson said with a chuckle. "Fetch the vases from my buggy, lass, and we'll see to the decorations."

She pointed to her buggy standing by the gate, and when I went over to it, the small bay mare with kind eyes whickered at me. I rubbed a hand over her velvet nose, then lifted four china pitchers out of the buggy and carried them to the table where Miss McPherson was lifting the flowers from her basket.

"It's a grand day for a tea and no mistake," she said when I arrived. "Can ye fill these with water?"

"Yes."

I took the pitchers two at a time and returned them, dripping and full, to Miss McPherson. Her hands were brown and strong looking, and her bent fingers moved among the flowers without hesitation, forming them into bunches. The green juice of the stems stained her lined fingernails.

"So ye love flowers?" she asked suddenly and I nodded.

"I used to have a garden," I told her. "My teacher helped me get it started."

"Oh aye. Where was this then?"

I began to tell her about the farm, about sweet peas and hollyhocks and nasturtiums, and as I talked she kept arranging her flowers and giving me bright glances. She reminded me of a bird — one of those small, rounded birds with soft plumage and bright, inquisitive eyes — and she smelled of lavender.

I told her about my garden getting wrecked by the pigs and she tutted her tongue. "Eh, that was a gey wicked thing," she sympathized. "And why are ye here at Hazelbrae House, Maggie?"

So then I told her about Thomasina, and about running away to find her.

"Mercy!" she exclaimed softly, once or twice. "And what will happen to ye next, Maggie?"

I fell silent and shrugged my shoulders, a cool shadow of anxiety dimming my happiness. Miss McPherson held my eyes with a long, considering glance. Then she patted my shoulder and gave it a sudden squeeze. "There's aye a solution for every problem," she said encouragingly. "Now, take these vases around and put one on each table, Maggie. And take my basket back to yon buggy. I must go and see Miss Weaver."

Only a few scattered petals and one curling leaf lay on the curved wood in the bottom of the basket. I returned it to the buggy, and gave the mare another pat. Her coat was hot and shiny, and she was stamping restlessly as other buggies came rolling up the road to Hazelbrae House.

Soon the garden was full. The mayor arrived and gave a speech about charity and good works and the duty of the citizens of Peterborough. A preacher stood on the verandah steps and gave grace, thanking God for the harvest tea and the hard work that had made it possible (I thought about us all darning socks and beating rugs) and asking God to be gracious to His servants and to bless their endeavors. My stomach rumbled, and I opened my eyes a crack to sneak a look around.

That was when I noticed Harold, wedged in at a table between two tall men in straw hats. My heart gave a leap, and at that moment Harold glanced up and looked right at me. He gave me a slow wink, and I squeezed my eyes shut again. Now the minister was talking about charity and generosity and diligence. I wondered if anyone would ever get to eat, but finally he finished. *Amen* swept through the crowd like wind over grass, then a babble of talk broke out. Girls scurried about with hot water for tea, and passed plates of scones, and ran to the kitchen to replenish the apple jelly. Laughing groups fanned out across the grass, the women's dresses sweeping around them, their parasols casting puddles of shade.

I looked frantically for Harold, and for Thomasina. I wanted Harold to see me first.

"Hey, Maggie," his voice said behind me, and when I turned there he was, taller and wider than I remembered. His smile was full of excitement and I felt my face glowing. I was so happy to see him; he was a piece of another part of my life, of me. "So, you ran away," he said admiringly. "I knew you could do it. Did you find Thomasina?"

"She's here somewhere," I said, but I didn't look

around for her. I wanted Harold to myself, and I was still a little scared that he might like her as much as he liked me, or that he wouldn't be able to tell us apart.

"I want to meet her," he said.

"How's Mae Beth?" I asked, changing the subject.

"She's here too," Harold said, "with Mother and Father." And he turned to scan the crowd. At that moment, we both saw her: Thomasina, carrying a plate of cake and heading in our direction. I bit my lip anxiously.

Thomasina paused at a group of ladies, then she crossed the grass towards me and I knew I would have to introduce her to Harold.

"Thomasina," he said, shaking her hand politely, like a grownup. His brown eyes smiled at her, and she offered him a piece of cake which he took, munching big hunks of it.

"Maggie's told me all about you," Harold said, and Thomasina laughed.

"I've heard all about you, too," she confessed.

Miss Weaver bustled past us. "Maggie, fetch more hot water," she called over her shoulder, "and Thomasina, keep the cake going around."

Thomasina made a face and told Harold she'd see him again, then she carried her plate towards another group of people. Playing children dashed past her, yelling, and disappeared around a corner of the house. Under the pine trees, Archie was raffling his painting and nearby a lady was selling quilts draped over a table. Someone had brought three fat ponies and was selling rides on them.

The ponies looked hot and bored, trudging around the yard with their heads low while children squirmed on their backs.

Harold munched his cake and suddenly I had to know what he was thinking.

"Is she like me?" I asked.

"Yes — and no," he said. "She doesn't smile the way you do, Maggie."

"I thought you would get us muddled up."

"No." Maybe he understood my anxiety. "*You're* the one who threw apples at me and put snow down my neck," he teased. "How could I get *you* muddled up with anyone?"

"Oh, Harold!" I swatted him on the shoulder and we started laughing. I felt giddy with relief. "You put snow down my neck, too!"

"I bloodied noses to defend you," he protested, "and all the time you were tougher than me."

"How do you like it, in town?" I asked.

"I love it!" he said enthusiastically. "I'm learning to make so many things, Maggie. And sometimes I ride Captain home to see everyone on the farm. I was wondering, Maggie, if you're allowed to go out? If I could borrow a buggy, I could take you around town and show you things. There's so much to see!"

"Yes," I replied, my face flushing. "But we'd have to ask Matron."

"Maggie!" interrupted a voice, and as I turned I was enveloped in a hug, a flurry of ruffles and beads and blonde curls.

"Mae Beth!"

"Oh, Maggie, we've been so worried about you! Let me look at you — are you all right? And I've met Thomasina already. She told me about your long walk and how a gentleman rescued you and painted a picture of you! And Mother had a letter from Mrs. Howard and she's staying in Toronto and Lizzy is having a great time with her cousins. And Willy has come here to town to work in a garage! And Mr. Howard is selling the farm and going down to Toronto and —"

"Slow down," I protested, laughing, as Mae Beth paused to draw breath.

"Tell us everything that's happened to you," Mae Beth commanded, and she linked her arm through mine.

We walked around the yard, amongst the strolling, laughing families. Harold paced beside us, swinging his hat and grinning at me, and I kept imagining riding in a buggy above Captain's chestnut back, while Harold held the reins in his strong fingers.

When we saw Thomasina nearby, I called her over and Mae Beth took her arm too. I didn't mind sharing my friends anymore; I knew suddenly that there was enough love in the world for Thomasina and me to each have a share. We walked around talking until Miss Weaver caught sight of us and bustled over to scold Thomasina and me back to work. Mae Beth gave me another hug, and told me she would try to visit me in town again. At the last minute, she pulled a small package from her pocket and handed it to me.

"I almost forgot!" she exclaimed. "This is for you."

I gave the package a shake; it rattled faintly. "What is it?"

"Seeds from your garden at the farm. I went there with Mother once, and I noticed some of the nasturtiums had seed pods on them. I got a hollyhock seed head, too. I thought I would plant them for you, next spring, but you can do it better yourself."

"Oh, Mae Beth!" I said, slipping the packet into my pocket happily.

"Maggie, Matron is waiting!" called Miss Weaver, and I gave Mae Beth a smile and went across the grass, dodging ladies' parasols and knots of playing children. On the front steps of the house, Miss Miller was organizing the orphan children into rows. It was time to perform the songs we had rehearsed all week.

Standing in the back row with Thomasina beside me, I opened my mouth wide and let the notes pour out. We sang *Onward Christian Soldiers* and *Rock of Ages; Red River Valley* and *My Bonnie Lies Over The Ocean*. This was a song that used to make me cry, but today nothing could shake my happiness. And anyway, Thomasina had *crossed* the ocean and was standing beside me, her mouth as wide open as mine. From the corner of my eye I could see her ribs moving up and down as she sang.

Too soon, it was time for the last song. Miss Miller had decided that Thomasina and I would sing it as a duet. The other children fell silent, and my legs began trembling under my long skirt. All week, I had been dreading this moment. The sea of faces gazed expectantly upwards, all their eyes focused only on Thomasina and me, burning holes in us. The faces swam in my vision, out of focus. In unison, Thomasina and I took a deep breath. When we opened our mouths the song slipped out, every note in its place, and I remembered our father's voice soaring over the women's hats in chapel, far away in the fishing town of St. Ives. He would be proud of us, his red haired daughters.

In the sea of faces, I saw Harold, his dark brown hair glinting with sunshine, his brown eyes fixed on me. I sang for him, for his friendship; and I sang for Mae Beth at his side. I sang for Thomasina, pressed against my shoulder, and I sang for Archie, who had befriended me on the road and who stood listening now beside his painting. I had heard that every raffle ticket had been sold. I sang for Miss McPherson in her blue dress, with her bright eyes steady on my face, and I sang to give thanks for everything that was beautiful: the blue sky, the hot sun, the flowers on the tables.

When Thomasina and I stopped, there was a deep hush and then a sudden storm of clapping. The sound beat about us, like wind. We turned to each other, flushed, triumphant, laughing with nerves. "We did it!" Thomasina said.

After that, the tea was over. People began to drift away in swirls, like leaves on a slow river. Matron stood at the gate and said goodbye to everyone, thanking them for coming. The minister put his black hat back on and climbed into a buggy hitched to a black horse, and Miss McPherson patted me on the shoulder as she left. "Remember, Maggie, there's aye a solution," she said warmly, and then Harold arrived to say goodbye. "That was *beautiful*," he said admiringly and I was tongue-tied and stupid, my heart jumping around.

"You've heard me sing before, lots of times," I said.

"But this was your public debut," he teased. "I'll let you know about a buggy. Bye, Maggie." He looked back at me twice on his way to the gate, and from the road he turned and waved.

Finally, as the last buggies rolled away, it was our turn to eat. We filed into the kitchen and jostled for places at the long tables. As a treat, there was jelly roll for dessert. Even Miss Weaver was in a good temper, and let us get away with more noise than usual. In the early dusk after supper, we straggled to and from the tea tables, carrying everything back inside: the stained cloths, crumpled doilies, wilting flowers, and dirty cutlery, the plates holding nothing but crumbs. Then the older boys dismantled the tables, and by dark the trampled grass was bare once more.

In my cot, I lay in the darkness, remembering every detail: Harold's admiring gaze, Mae Beth's laughter, Miss McPherson's bushel basket of flowers, like a bushel of light. I thought of all the things I had hauled around the farm in bushel baskets: pig food and kindling wood, apples and weeds to throw over the pasture fence, cobs of corn and wet laundry. I will not return to that, I thought with determination. I will be like Miss McPherson and carry flowers around. One day, I will have my flower shop.

Thomasina reached out her arm and I met it halfway;

we clutched hands between our cots. "Father would have been proud of our singing," she whispered, speaking my own thoughts aloud as she often did. I squeezed her hand. I knew that we had sounded just right, singing together in the late afternoon sun.

Now, I felt as though my heart was still singing, and brim full of light like the basket of flowers.

CHAPTER
SEVENTEEN

Three days after the harvest tea, Miss Miller, the matron, called me to her office. I dried my wet hands, and followed her down the hall. Thomasina glanced up from her desk as I passed; I saw her anxious look. She's sending me away, I thought as I followed Matron's silent steps and her swinging, dark blue hem. Now the tea is over, she's going to tell me to pack. A buggy will come for me and carry me down miles of silent dusty roads to a farm on a hill. I won't see Thomasina again.

My stomach clenched tight, my throat closed.

Matron's door swung silently shut behind me on its oiled hinges, the sun gleaming on its oak panels. Matron sat down at her desk and turned over some papers while I stood waiting against the door. My own breathing filled my ears.

Finally she looked up. "Maggie, I have had a letter from Mrs. Howard in Toronto," she said. "She writes that you worked well and hard on the Howards' farm, and her sister has added a postscript praising you for your action in getting help when Mrs. Howard was unwell."

The letter rustled in Matron's hand. Blood roared in my ears.

"You can't send me back to the farm!" I blurted out. "Mr. Howard is selling it!"

Matron gave me a sharp, inquiring glance. "The letter says nothing of that," she said. "But I wasn't considering sending you back there, Maggie. It wouldn't be suitable when only men are left. Nonetheless, you need to go somewhere."

I gulped noisily. I was sure Matron must have heard me. My hands clenched together and I tried to relax them and let them hang by my sides. "Please don't send me far away," I pleaded. "I need to be close to Thomasina so I can still see her."

Matron's gaze softened. "You have waited many years to be together," she agreed. "Maggie, how about working in town as a domestic help? Your duties would involve cooking and cleaning, laying fires, buying groceries, and taking care of laundry."

"I've done all those things on the farm!" I said. Oh, please, *please*, I thought, let me stay in town. Then I will be close to Thomasina. And Harold.

"There is a doctor in town, who lives near Hazelbrae House," Matron resumed. "He is an older man, who is widowed. His sister has come to live with him, and she has asked me to send her a girl to help in the house. The previous domestic recently left. I've arranged for the doctor's sister to collect you this afternoon, Maggie. Miss Weaver will give you a supply of clothes to take with you. You may go and find her now."

"Yes," I said. I wiped my sweating hands on my dress and rushed down the hall to find Thomasina. "Listen," I said breathlessly. "I'm going away, but not far, just nearby to a house in town!"

Her anxious eyes softened.

"I have to go this afternoon — they're coming for me," I explained. I knew I was lucky, but still — how could I say goodbye to Thomasina? How could I lie alone at night in the house of strangers, while somewhere, in the same city, Thomasina lay alone in her cot?

"Maggie, we'll still see each other," she said soberly, and she caught my hand and gripped it hard.

I nodded. "I know. I have to go and find Miss Weaver now."

Miss Weaver fussed about my clothes. She told me how to wash and care for each item, she folded and unfolded things, she lectured me about how lucky I was to be so well provided for. I listened to her through a fog of anxiety. What would this doctor's sister be like, I wondered? I remembered Kathleen Howard rocking in her parlor while I struggled to keep the house clean. But surely a doctor's sister would be better organized, and surely a town house would be easier to keep clean than a farmhouse?

"You're not listening to a word I'm saying!" complained Miss Weaver in exasperation, and she sent me off to polish spoons in the kitchen.

The morning dragged by, the hands on the white clock barely moving. I wondered what time the doctor's sister would come for me; I wanted to know the exact moment. I couldn't stand the suspense, the huge weight of all the unknown possibilities. I felt as if a door had opened in my life, but that beyond that door everything was dark. I wanted to see through the darkness. I needed to know if the doctor would be stern or kind; if his sister would be strict; if I would have a room of my own; how far away the house was to which they would take me. My stomach curled and uncurled nervously, like a nest of snakes.

At lunch, I pressed my shoulder hard against Thomasina, slurping my vegetable broth, missing her already. They would have to let us visit each other. I would refuse to work if they didn't. I would fuss and complain. I would run away and tell Matron I wanted to work somewhere else. When I glanced sideways at Thomasina, I saw that her chin was in the air and her face was pale. I knew that she would fuss too, that no one could keep us apart ever again.

After lunch, Miss Weaver placed my trunk of clothes near the door. I couldn't believe my eyes when I saw it — it was the very same one I had left behind on the Howards' farm. Miss Weaver said that the Barnardo home visitor had fetched it back for me. I put my flour sack, with the seashells, and the flower seeds Mae Beth had brought me, inside the trunk with my clothes. Miss Weaver gave me a cloth and I polished the stair banister and spindles while I waited for the doctor's sister to come for me. I thought I might be sick. Thomasina kept poking her face around the office door, looking worried.

"Here she comes," said Miss Weaver suddenly, when I

was up at the top of the stairs, and I was so startled that I dropped my polishing cloth on the floor and left it lying there. I was halfway down the stairs when Miss Weaver opened the front door and the doctor's sister walked inside.

"Well, Maggie, are ye all ready then?" she asked, her bright eyes considering me kindly.

"Miss McPherson!" I cried, surprise and happiness rushing over me. I just knew that Miss McPherson would be kind and wise, that her house would be easy to keep clean. I was so happy that I hugged her, and with a chuckle she hugged me back.

"Maggie!" remonstrated Miss Weaver sharply, but I didn't care.

"Dinna fash yerself, Maggie and I are old friends," Miss McPherson told her. "And here's your bonny twin sister, Maggie, come to say goodbye."

I hugged Thomasina hard, hard, feeling her hipbones and her ribs against mine. "It's Miss McPherson, who brought the flowers!" I told her. "It's going to be fine, Thomasina!"

"Aye, we'll be arranging visits between the two of ye, soon enough," said Miss McPherson. "It's no right to separate the likes of you. Miss Weaver, I'll be calling on Matron later this week. Tell her I'm all for taking Thomasina out every Sunday afternoon to spend time with Maggie."

"Certainly," said Miss Weaver formally, and then two boys arrived to carry my trunk to the buggy. I followed Miss McPherson's scent of lavender out through the door to where the mare with kind brown eyes waited patiently. Thomasina ran to the gate. We waved until trees cut off our view of each other.

"It's no so far away ye'll be," comforted Miss McPherson. "This is our street already."

I glanced at the street sign: Benson.

"I've been here!" I cried. "I came this way when I walked south to find Thomasina!"

"Aye, like enough," agreed Miss McPherson. "And here's the dear doctor's house, where ye'll help me out. My old hands and back are no so strong as they used to be."

My mouth hung open.

"*Here*?" I squeaked. "I'm going to live *here*?"

Although the fall grass had lost its bright green color, and although almost all the flowers had finished blooming, I recognized the house immediately. I remembered how I had leaned on the fence weeks ago, staring at the sweet peas and sunflowers in the garden, at the blue shutters on the house, at the horse hanging its head over the blue barn door. "It's my dream house," I said wonderingly.

Miss McPherson laughed. "Aye, I thought ye'd like the garden right enough," she said. "Next summer ye can help me plant and till it, Maggie."

In a daze, I climbed from the buggy, while a boy ran out of the house next door and took the mare away to unhitch her. I followed Miss McPherson to the back door of my dream house.

"The doctor's in his study," she told me. "We'll just

give him a wee glimpse of ye."

I followed her through the house. It smelled of lavender and polish and soup simmering on the stove. Blue
curtains, with flower patterns, framed the windows in
soft folds. The polished wood floors lay smooth and
bright, splashes of sunshine gleamed in copper pans and
a vase of flowers flared into brilliance on a table. This
was nothing like the farmhouse, with its dim rooms and
dingy floors and dark colors. Everything in the doctor's
house was clean and licked with brightness.

Miss McPherson knocked on a closed door and
entered with me behind her. The man in the leather
chair swiveled from his desk and surveyed me over the
gold rims of his spectacles. "Oh, it's the new lass," he
said. "Maggie, the runaway."

I didn't know if he was teasing me or not, but then he
smiled, creasing the lines in his face deeper. His eyes
were bright and curious and kind, like his sister's eyes.
His hair was like hers too, thick and wavy and pure
white, and his eyebrows were clumps of snowy bristles.
"A lass with some spunk," he said.

"Aye, she'll not need to worry about all that now,"
Miss McPherson said comfortably. "Don't go teasing
her. She's coming to have a cup of tea."

"Verra good," the doctor agreed, adjusting his glasses.
"Two women in my office at once is more than my old
heart can stand." His eyes twinkled at me before he bent
back over his desk. Behind him, the wall was lined with
heavy books.

"Come," Miss McPherson said, and I followed her to

the kitchen with its bubbling soup and gleaming wood stove.

"Dinna heed the dear doctor," she said. "He's an awful tease."

I nodded, and then I noticed it — hanging over the table, signed by Archie.

"You got the picture!" I cried. "The picture of Thomasina and me in the garden!"

"Aye, happen I did. 'Twas my number that won the raffle at the harvest tea."

"It's like having Thomasina here, too," I said.

"Aye, she's not so far away. A few minutes walk for your long legs. Take your tea out into the sunshine, Maggie. When ye've drunk it, I'll show ye your room and your tasks in the house."

I sat on the verandah in a white wicker chair, sipping sweet, strong tea in a china cup. The horse in the blue barn turned its head to watch me, its ears flicking back and forth. A tabby cat came silently up the steps and jumped into my lap, and I rubbed it behind the ears until it purred.

Fall sunshine warmed the cat's coat and my knees, and gleamed in the last sunflowers in the garden. Their heavy heads drooped; their petals were chips of light. Next spring, I thought, I will help make this garden beautiful again — and Thomasina and Harold can visit me here. On Sunday afternoons we can sit on a blanket and watch the roses come into bloom. I will grow my nasturtium and hollyhock seeds, from my garden on the farm. One day, I will have a flower shop here in town.

When Miss McPherson opened the door and carried her own tea outside, the cat glanced up with golden eyes. Miss McPherson smiled at me. "Aye, ye've made another new friend," she said, and the cat purred even louder.

DATE DUE

MAR 1 9 2002	

BRODART, CO.   Cat. No. 23-221-003